THE IMAGE OF ME

a novel

For Jan ~
What a joy being
in Exercise class
together!
All the best ~
Karin Cutler
12.17.19

KARIN CUTLER

First edition, 2019.

For Ed, Mike, Dan, Andy, and Kenny.

Cutler Strong.

"You are not truly living and giving
if you deny what is in your heart."

THE IMAGE OF ME

1

A BLACK VELVET SKY cloaked the small community of Willow Springs, New Mexico. Sequin stars dotted the darkness. An opalescent moon illuminated the mountains beyond the state park on the far side of town. Its light radiated across the central square and surrounding neighborhoods. In her modest adobe home, Mim Rodriguez's heart-wrenching cries woke her from her sleep.

"Mom?" Her daughter crept into the room and sat on the bed. "You're having another nightmare."

"Nini," Mim rolled toward her. "The lizards. Rosie was chasing the lizards down the path and I couldn't catch her."

"It's okay." Nini smoothed the wild chestnut hair over her mother's sweat-drenched forehead.

"But I couldn't save her."

"It's not your fault," Nini said. "It was just a dream. Try to get some sleep." She tucked the comforter around her mother's shoulders. "Dad will be here tonight for my celebration dinner." She touched her lips to the top of her mother's head.

Back in her room, Nini collapsed onto the bed, expelling a huff of air. She sat up on her elbow and reached for the picture on her nightstand. “Rosie,” she said to the impish three year old, “Will she ever love me as much as she loved you?”

The frosted blender of margaritas whirred to a stop. Mim piled handfuls of crispy chips on a pottery plate and poured chunky salsa in the center bowl. She glanced again out the kitchen window.

Nini joined her. “I thought Dad would be here by now.”

Mim nodded at her phone on the counter. “He texted forty-five minutes ago that he’s on his way. I’ve been watching for him.”

“I’m worried about you, Mom,” Nini said. “I think we should talk to Dad about your nightmares.” She dipped a chip in the salsa. “I bet if you weren’t sleeping alone…” She eyed her mother.

“We’ve been over this. It’s more complicated than that.”

“Mom, I mean he should marry you. He and Eva have been divorced three years now. What’s wrong with him? He loves you, right?”

“Yes, but…”

“And you love him.”

“It’s not that simple.”

“Right, he’s got the twins. But they’re in middle school now. Besides, what about me? I deserve to have a dad too.”

Tires crunched on the gravel driveway. "There he is." Nini popped another chip in her mouth and dashed out the front door.

Mim paused at the window. She watched Rod, Armando Rodriguez, Jr., slick his coal black hair off his forehead, a habit she still found endearing. He caught his daughter in his arms, lifted her off her feet, and handed her a single pink rose.

"Thanks, Dad," Nini kissed his cheek. "I'll go put this in some water." She brushed past Mim who stood in the doorway.

Rod licked his lips and grinned. "For you," he said. He held out a bouquet of gerber daisies and slipped his other arm around Mim's waist.

"Thank you," she brushed her lips against his.

Nini emerged from the kitchen. "I was just telling Mom I think it would be great if you two..."

Mim cleared her throat. "I've got chips and margaritas ready. Let's go out back."

Nini brought iced tea and they gathered around the table under the covered patio. Rod raised his glass, "To our daughter's first day of high school."

"To our daughter," Mim clinked her glass with theirs and looked at Rod, "You should see her new outfit."

"I'll model it for you." Nini zipped in the back door.

"She's growing up too fast," Rod shook his head. "Before we know it, she'll be off to college."

College, thought Mim, *leaving me alone.*

“What do you think, Dad?” Nini danced onto the patio, twirling in her black skirt and striped tunic top.

Déjà vu, Mim thought. “I’ll be back in a minute.” She went to the closet in her room. She swept her clothes aside and regarded the portfolios behind them like lost friends. She picked out the maroon folder and rifled through her early work. Picture in hand, she returned to the patio. “Remember this?” She held out the drawing for Nini and Rod.

“Is that me?” Nini squinted her eyes.

“Yup, you were, what,” Rod looked up at Mim, “four years old?”

Mim nodded. “Showing off your new Easter dress.”

“And who is that handsome man?” Rod said.

“That handsome man was a cocky baseball star,” Mim said. “If his teammates hadn’t dared him to pose for my Life Drawing class, we may never have met.”

Rod leaned toward Nini. “Your mom couldn’t take her eyes off me,” he whispered.

“Ew!” Nini scrunched her face.

“I think I have that portrait.” Mim ran back to her room and returned with the portfolio. She flipped through the sketches. “Here it is.” She winked at Rod.

Nini examined the drawing of Rod in his college baseball uniform. “Rodriguez. Number Twelve,” Nini read the back of the jersey. “Look at that hair hanging out of your helmet.” She handed the picture to her dad.

She peeked over Mim's shoulder, "Wow Mom, the entrance to Soaring Eagle State Park. I love it. That eagle looks like it might fly right off the page."

Rod gazed at Mim with warmth in his eyes. *You still have it.*

She recalled their first date at the restaurant at Peaceful Pines. They were sitting on the patio sipping wine when they spotted two eagles soaring above the trees. He had taken her hand. "Our totem. You and I soaring together. No harm can come to us."

"Oh, what happened to it?" Nini said. "Looks like it's been torn."

Mim's heart froze. She could not look at Rod. She flipped through the pages. Nini plucked another picture from the file and giggled. "Look at this, Dad. Grandma Irene in her apron."

"Don't laugh. Your mom got an award for a drawing like that. You know the one. In Grandma's kitchen?"

"Grandma in her apron and Grandpa in his art smock?"

"It was for Career Day." Mim said.

"Grandma loves aprons," Nini said. "She made the one you wear, didn't she, Mom?" Mim nodded. "I wonder if I still have that apron she made for me when I was little."

"I think it's in one of the boxes in the garage," Mim said.

"Oh hey," Nini pointed, "is that...?"

Mim passed over the drawing of toddler Nini, peering over the dashboard of Joseph Begay's truck, her arm around his puppy on the seat beside her. She stopped at a sketch of Rod's mom, Yoli. "How about this one?" she said.

Nini took the page from her mother. "That can't be Nana. She's so young."

"It is," Mim said.

"Oh, sweet baby," Nini cooed. "Is that Rosie?"

"That's you," Rod said, "see the date? 2003."

2003, the year Rosie died.

Mim put the glasses on the tray. "Who's hungry?" she said. "Let's go celebrate!"

2

MIM SAT A MOMENT before starting the car. She blinked her eyes and rolled her shoulders, laced her fingers and stretched toward the steering wheel. She had not slept well, disturbed by the exchange between Rod and Nini last night.

"It's time to head home," Rod had said. "How about a hug?"

"You could be home, Dad," Nini had said. "Maybe then Mom's nightmares would stop."

He had looked at Mim with hurt in his eyes. He whispered, "I wish you would have told me," brushed his lips against hers, and left.

Mim turned out of her neighborhood. Her heart softened at the sight of the sky above the mountains, a parfait of blues layered with whipped cream clouds. The Town Square was quiet. On the corner across from the Splash Pad, the sun glimmered off the window of Cactus Coffee. Oversized planters stood guard on either side of the stained glass front door.

She parked on the side street in front of the brown metal door displaying the peach logo of Fit Fanny, her dear friend, Silkie Mercer's, exercise studio. Mim jangled her keys in the lock and entered the hallway, inhaling the aroma of coffee beans.

She unlocked the back door to the coffee shop and flipped the light switch. A cactus border paraded around the ivory walls atop the cardinal red chair rail. The sage green tables complemented the rust-colored Saltillo tile floor.

Mim secured her purse in the back room where the fridge rumbled and grabbed her apron from the hook behind the door. She filled a couple of coffee pots with water, scooped fresh grounds into the coffee machine and pressed, "Brew."

The hallway door shut. Then a rough voice, "Good morning, Mim." Silkie appeared, untying the wrap-around skirt she wore over her peach workout capris.

"How was the Back-to-School Breakfast?"

"One of my favorite events of the year. I'm glad they still invite me."

"Being the principal's wife and event coordinator might help," Mim said.

"I ran into Nini. She's such a doll. How'd dinner go last night?"

"She told Rod I'm having nightmares again." Mim rearranged the mugs on the shelf. "And that she thinks I'd sleep better if I weren't sleeping alone."

Her friend raised her eyebrows. "Now that's..."

"Silkie," Addy Freeman poked her head into the shop. "Let's get moving. I need to keep this body in shape," she slid her hands over her hips.

"Good morning to you, too," Mim said to the wall.

Silkie rolled her eyes, wagging a finger at Mim, "This conversation is not over."

Mim glanced at the clock, "6:55." She retrieved the remote from the counter and lowered the awning, shading the shop from the morning sun. She looked around to be sure everything was in order and turned the sign in the front window to "OPEN."

Mim had just made her way back to the counter when the chime of bells on the front door announced the Morning Men, Chet Phillips, Ralph Haynes, and Benny Orozco, the three regulars who had been coming to the shop since Mim opened.

"Good morning, Mim," Ralph greeted her, his eyes, one brown and one blue, twinkled in his handsome face, his beard, a runoff of his full head of milky white hair, neatly trimmed.

"Smells good in here," Chet Phillips, his once blond flat top now sprinkled with gray, passed by the counter. His subtle limp was a reminder of his service in Vietnam.

Benny Orozco, owner of El Corral Mexican Restaurant, stopped a moment, his robust frame looming over the counter. "Is Nini excited about school today?" he said. "My Nico's so nervous he hardly slept a wink." Benny was in charge of sending the last of his six children off to school. He stopped by for coffee before joining his wife at the restaurant to prep for the day's meals.

They selected their mugs from the collection on the back shelf. Mim met them at their table in the corner by the front window with a pot of coffee and a plate of pastries.

After class, the exercise ladies moseyed through the back door, placed their orders, and proceeded to a table in the middle of the shop. When Mim was delivering their coffee, she heard Benny's deep voice from the men's table, "Look at that Addy." Mim glanced up as Addy eased the band from her ponytail, fluffing her shimmering blond hair over her shoulders.

"Doesn't she have a bounce in her step these days?"

Mim eyed her. *She does*, Mim hated to agree.

"I stopped to see her dad yesterday and he told me..." Mim strained to hear Chet's response.

"Oh," Karyl Stevens settled into her chair and frowned at her cell phone. "I was hoping I'd hear from Ali. They posted the students in this year's Vietnam Project this morning."

"I'm sure she made it," Chet's wife, Ellen, said. "She's so smart and..."

"She's number one in her class," Karyl said, "and co-captain of the girls' swim team. Not to mention the clubs she belongs to." Ellen looked at Addy, who tried to hide a grin. "You know she volunteers at the nursing home so she can spend time with Great-Grandpa Fred. She's worried about him, though. Lately he's been calling her Alice."

Ellen nodded. "I'm not surprised, at his age. Imagine spending every day with someone for over seventy years and then they're gone. How can you prepare for that?" She looked over at the Morning Men and was quiet a moment. She smiled. "Chet and I have been married forty years. I'd be lost without him."

“Speaking of lost,” Silkie sipped her latte, “don’t tell me Marie went to babysit her grandchildren again. I told her she should stay home and take care of her husband.” She set her cup down. “She’s probably going to miss Rhonda’s sex toy party, too.”

“That’s tomorrow night,” Ellen said. “She asked me to take notes.”

Chairs scraped the tile as the Morning Men rose from their table. Chet placed his hands on his wife’s shoulders, “You ready, Honey?”

Silkie leaned on the counter on her way to the studio. ”About your nightmares, Mim. Do you think counseling might help?” Cups clanked in the sink. “I like Nini’s idea, too.” She winked.

Mim blushed. She liked that option better.

Mim was in the kitchen preparing Nini’s favorite green chile enchiladas when she heard her cell phone. There’s Nini. Mim read the text, “Having dinner at Grace’s, OK?” Grace Vega and Nini were like sisters. Mim had met Grace’s mom, Hortensia, at the neighborhood park when she and Nini moved to Willow Springs. Hortensia stayed at home with her three little ones and she volunteered to babysit.

Disappointed, Mim popped the casserole in the oven and decided to go for a walk while it cooked. She drove east to the state park. When Mim was offered the job as Education Coordinator there thirteen years ago she knew it was a sign that she and Rod would get back together. She passed the sculpture of the eagle at the entrance to the park reminding her of the sadness in Rod's eyes last evening. Her heart ached.

A truck with the park logo on the door was in the lot outside the Education Center. Mim thought of the six years she had worked there when Joseph Begay was park superintendent. She had been dazzled by his tall, muscular stature and intimidated by his formality during her interview. It was more than a year before they had a personal conversation. Mim smiled as she recalled two year old Nini playing on the floor with her toys when a gangly German shepherd puppy loped into the office, landing a slobbery kiss on her cheek just as Joseph appeared, a horrified look on his face. Nini squealed with delight and Bandit flopped down beside her.

Mim parked at the two-mile loop, donned her visor, grabbed her water bottle, and set off down the trail. Her thoughts returned to last evening, as they had all day. How she enjoyed their dinner celebration. When Nini went to the bathroom, Rod teased, "She'll be gone soon. You don't have to be alone, you know." She rubbed his thigh under the table. She knew she loved him. She knew he wanted to marry her. She knew Nini deserved a family. But was Mim ready? Could she put her guilt behind her?

Mim stopped for a moment at a small picnic area. What should she do? She leaned back against the cement slab. Her heart stopped. In the sky above, two eagles soared.

Startled by the crunch of footsteps on the path, she sat up. Joseph? She watched him stride toward her, his rugged body belying his fifty-plus years. His long black hair highlighted his comely face beneath his park ranger hat. "Joseph," she hopped off the bench, "what are you doing here?"

"Meet the new superintendent," he reached his arms out.

"You're back?" she parried his advance, sparks in her eyes. "Why didn't you tell me?"

"There was so much to do in two short weeks. Loose ends up north. Moving. A phone call seemed so hollow. I wanted to tell you..."

"When you could find the time?" She dismissed him and stomped down the trail.

"I needed to see your eyes light up." His words carried away on the wind.

Mim fumed the whole way home. *Joseph, back. How could he not tell me? When he was here in May, he mentioned wanting to return. And Silkie had to know,* Mim thought. *She's on the park board of directors. But she was a sealed vault when it came to secrets.*

She was comforted by the aroma of the green chile enchiladas baking in the oven. Her timing was perfect. She spooned cookie dough onto a baking sheet and put it in the oven.

Mim went to her room, tossed her damp shirt and shorts into the laundry basket, and reached for the caftan in her closet. Tucked beneath was the portfolio from last night. She fingered through the drawings. There it is. She lifted the torn picture of the soaring eagle. Guilt weighed heavy upon her. *I'll restore it and surprise Rod,* she thought.

She spied the thin black folder where she concealed her private collection and thumbed through until she found her first portrait of Rod. She peered at it, a looking glass into the past. Advanced Life Drawing class. Her first year at the university. Mim took her place at her easel amidst the elite circle of classmates, spectators in the studio arena. She tamed her chestnut hair in a red print scarf and laid out her supplies in anticipation of this week's subject.

The sun beamed through the window, a spotlight on the figure of the daunting gladiator before them. Mim was mesmerized. The metallic black hair, a helmet protecting his angular face; the fierce steely eyes; and the lips. Oh my. Mim hid her grin. She looked at her array of colored pencils. She would have to create an x-rated mauve for those lips, the perfect contrast to the luscious honey color of his sculpted torso and legs. She was so absorbed in capturing his commanding presence, she was spooked when the instructor whispered, "Class is over." The gladiator gave a victorious wink. She stashed her supplies in her tote and raced out.

Two days later, Mim was studying in the Student Union when she felt an imposing presence behind her. A finger tapped her paper. "Mim Johnstone," a husky voice read. She raised her eyes, her heart caught in her throat. The Gladiator.

"The artist, right?" His hand grazed her kinky hair. She blushed. "Armando Rodriguez, Jr.," he offered his hand, "my friends call me Rod." He nodded toward his teammates, who stood nearby, catlike grins on their faces.

The sound of the buzzer intruded on her reverie. She slipped the drawing back into the portfolio and returned to the kitchen. The cookies were done. She set the cookie sheet on the cooling rack and slid the second batch into the oven. She was about to spoon the enchiladas onto her plate when her cell phone rang. Rod. "I was just sitting down to dinner," she said. "How was your day?"

"Good. I had the boys over. They just left. How did Nini's first day go?"

"I haven't seen her yet. She's having dinner with Grace."

"So you are eating alone? I have a solution for that. Join me for dinner next week, say, Tuesday?"

"I would like that," Mim said.

"Just the two of us," Rod said.

Mim heard noise in the background, then the voice of Eva, Rod's ex, "Rod? I forgot to tell you..."

Eva? The muscles in Mim's neck tightened and she stabbed the "hang up" icon on her phone.

"Mom?" Nini sauntered into the kitchen, backpack flung over her shoulder. "Mmm, smells good in here."

"Thanks, green chile enchiladas and..."

"Grandma's chocolate drop cookies? My favorites." She twirled on her tippy toes.

"So how was your first day?"

"Interesting. Give me a minute to put my backpack away and we can talk on the patio."

Mim slathered chocolate icing on the fresh cookies. Her phone dinged. Rod. She ignored it and joined Nini at the patio table. The sun was just going down and the evening was still warm. Nini took a bite of her cookie and licked the chocolate frosting from her lips.

"Tell me about your day," Mim said. She placed a cookie in front of her and broke off a piece.

"Great day. Just..." Nini swiped her finger across the frosting on another cookie. "I don't know how to explain it. This has never happened before."

"Of course not. High school's not like middle school."

"It's not that. It's, well, you know how on the first day the teacher reads all the names out loud. I was okay in the first class. Ms. Linstrom said, 'Cynthia Rodriguez.' I said, Here, it's Nini. People call me Nini. That was fine. Then in Block Two, Mr. Washburn said, 'Cynthia Rodriguez.' I said, it's Nini. And, Mom, I had the strangest feeling. Like, yes, me, I'm Nini. Not Cynthia. Nini. Because Rosie called me Nini."

"She couldn't say Cynthia. She called you Nini."

"In her sweet little voice," Nini said with Mim. Her parents always said that, "in her sweet little voice," when they told the story. Mim smiled.

"I know this sounds funny, but I felt her there, like she's part of me, like I'm Nini because my sister said so. It made me feel special."

Nini retired to her room and picked up the photo of Rosie as she always did. “I’ve always felt you here,” she looked around the room, “but today I felt you here.” She pressed the photo to her heart and curled under the covers.

In her room, Mim smiled and wrapped her arms around her shoulders. How she cherished these fleeting moments of intimacy with her daughter. She lifted the comforter, climbed into bed, and felt for the velvet pouch under her pillow. She caressed the letters embroidered on the front, “FOREVER.”

3

MIM ARRIVED AT THE coffee shop early on Thursday trying to avoid Silkie. She felt left out even though she knew Silkie would never share someone else's news. But this was Joseph. Mim breathed in the aroma of the brewing coffee and looked at the clock. Her friend was running late.

When Silkie poked her head in the back door, Mim greeted her, "Good morning, I was starting to worry about you."

"Fell back asleep after Tom left. How'd Nini's first day go?"

"She was so excited, she had to tell me all about it. We sat on the patio..."

Silkie's mind drifted to a time long ago. The beloved "mother and daughter on the patio" scene.

"You're pregnant, Silkie?" Beer had spewed from her mother's mouth. "I was sure you'd die a virgin." She laughed so loudly, Silkie knew the neighbors could hear. She clenched her fists. *Why did I think she might feel something for me?*

"He wants to marry you? He can have you." Silkie had married, miscarried, and divorced. A year later, she married Tom and they moved to Willow Springs.

"... a ride tonight? Silkie?" Mim shook her friend's arm.

"Oh, sorry, I got lost in my thoughts. Must need my morning mocha."

Mim squirted white chocolate syrup into a mug. She leaned closer and whispered, "Can I get a ride to Rhonda's party?"

"Her sex toy party?" Silkie blurted, "I thought you weren't going."

"I have a date with Rod next week."

"Ooh. Pick you up just before 6:00."

4

MIM LOOKED AROUND CACTUS COFFEE at the early morning crowd. She felt, what did Nini say at breakfast this morning? "Confident." That was it. She felt confident. She pulled her shoulders back and held her head up. She had allowed herself to relax and join in the fun with the women at Rhonda's party last evening. She felt like she belonged.

Mim waved at Marie and Karyl, dressed in their exercise outfits. If you could call Karyl's an exercise outfit. She looked like she could go right to the mall after class. "Good morning, Ladies. When did you get back, Marie?"

"Late yesterday."

"You missed Rhonda's party. She had a great selection. Something for everyone."

Ellen came through the back door and embraced Marie. "I've missed you."

Karyl made a face. "I'm going on to class," she said.

Ellen looped her arm through Marie's and escorted her out.

Mim looked up as Joseph entered the shop. "So much for a good mood," she mumbled.

"Hey Joseph," Ralph called from the Morning Men's table, "I heard you were back."

Mim waited behind the counter. "I'm surprised to see you this morning. Seems the guys knew you were back," she motioned to the corner.

"I thought you'd be in a better mood after all the fun you ladies had at Rhonda's last night."

She gave him the "How do you know about Rhonda's?" look.

"I was keeping Bob company next door while Addy was at the sex toy party."

Mim blushed at the way he said sex toy party. "I didn't know you and Dr. Freeman were friends."

"Going on thirty years now. I check in on him, especially since his fall."

Mim was curious about his relationship with Bob, but she knew that was all he was going to say. "What can I get you this morning? Your usual?"

Joseph nodded, his attention diverted to the exercise ladies prancing into the coffee shop. Mim handed him his steaming cup as Addy strutted past, brushing her breasts against him, a provocative look in her eyes. Joseph peeked down her v-neck top.

"Careful, it's hot," Mim said.

"Hey, looks like Fred Stevens escaped again," Silkie pointed toward the Square.

"Will you call the nursing home, please?" Joseph said, striding toward the door. "Tell them I'll bring him home."

Karyl sighed and shook her head. "Thanks, Joseph, I've got him," she said.

"Looks like we're too late," Joseph opened the door and motioned across the street. Judith Wilmott had arrived with her students from the high school.

"Ali," Karyl called. Her daughter was already enfolded in Grandpa Fred's arms. Behind them, a girl dressed in black with short spiky hair, wrapped her arms around her shoulders and swayed back and forth, mimicking them.

"Chloe," Judith admonished her.

Joseph passed by Bob's on his way to Soaring Eagle. There was a gray pickup in the driveway. Frankie's truck. He smiled and drove on.

5

MIM RINSED HER COFFEE CUP in the sink and looked out the window at the powder blue New Mexico sky. She grabbed a dish towel as Ruben Vega pulled into the driveway in his pickup, a hand-me-down from his dad on his sixteenth birthday. Nini hopped out of the truck, threw her backpack over her shoulder, and waved as he backed out.

"I'm not used to Ruben driving," Mim met Nini at the door. "I remember you kids playing soccer in the street."

"Must've done some good, Mom, he's on the high school team now." She hugged her mother. "Are you ready to do some damage at the mall?" Nini nodded at Mim's purse by the door. "Let me put my backpack away."

Mim listened as Nini talked about her sleepover at Grace's and her first week of classes during the forty-five minute drive. "Have you had any problems with the upperclassmen?"

"I don't know why I worried all summer. They don't even come to the freshmen wing. Besides when you're friends with the soccer team," she smiled at her mom. "How are things at the coffee shop? Anything new?"

Joseph is back, Mim wanted to say. There was a day when Nini would have been overjoyed that the man she once asked to be her grandfather was back. But three years after Joseph transferred to a park up north, Rod and Eva divorced. "Now Dad can marry you and we can be a family again," Nini had said.

"Nothing too exciting," Mim said. "Fred Stevens was at the square in his pajamas yesterday."

Nini giggled. "He was wandering around the PE field Thursday. Mr. Mercer let him eat lunch in the cafeteria before Ali took him back. I think he likes sneaking out. It's like a Willow Springs game, 'Where's Grandpa Fred?' If you find him, you get to take him back to the nursing home."

The mall had just opened when they arrived and Mim found a parking spot near their favorite department store. Nini perused the sales racks and found several tops, shorts, and jeans to try. She pulled out a slinky sundress. "What do you think of this, Mom?" she said.

"I wouldn't let you out of the house in that."

"Not for me, for you."

Mim looked down at her boxy tee and capris. She thought of Addy. And Rod. *Time to sass up my wardrobe.* She picked out several possibilities including a bright yellow low-cut tank top. "How about this?" she asked Nini. "Too low?" She motioned across her chest.

"Ooh, Mom, Dad will love that," Nini said, as they went to try them on. They had their own little fashion show, strutting in front of the fitting room mirrors.

Nini's stomach growled. Lunchtime. On the way to the Food Court, they passed a trendy children's shop where a little girl in a flowered dress twirled on her toes. "Look Daddy." He swooped her up in his strong arms. She squealed.

"Must be something about little girls dancing with their fathers," Nini said, thinking of the drawing of her and Rod. "Let's go back and buy that sexy dress and Dad can take you dancing."

After lunch, they finished shopping and trudged to the car, laden with their purchases. "Whew, I'm tired," Mim said, climbing into the driver's seat. "I'm looking forward to a quiet evening."

"Um, Mom," Nini said, "Ruben invited me to go to the park tonight. Since you're tired..."

"What's going on at the park?"

"Some of the guys from the soccer team are hanging out. He said it's a lot of fun."

"I'm sure it is, but these boys are older than you. Is Grace going?"

"She has to babysit, but..."

"I'm not comfortable with you going out there, especially if Grace isn't going."

"I knew you'd say that. Can I at least go to Grace's to help her babysit?"

"I guess so," Mim said, "as long as you're home by ten."

"Ten?" Nini's eyes rolled back in her head. She folded her arms across her chest and stared out the passenger window.

MIM INHALED THE AROMA of coffee brewing. She wrapped herself in her robe and padded to the kitchen.

"You're up early," she kissed Nini on the cheek. "I thought you'd sleep in. You went right to bed when you came home last night." She poured her coffee. Nini put the finishing touches on their traditional Sunday breakfast of French toast smothered in maple syrup and crispy bacon strips. They took their plates to the patio. The warmth of the September sun seeped through the cool morning air.

"Mmm, delicious," Mim savored a forkful of buttery French toast. "Did those little ones wear you out last night?"

"Not too bad. We played awhile and they went to bed. Juanito was engrossed in his video games."

"How'd Grace like your new outfit?"

"Oh, uh, she loved it. I told her she should get Hortensia to take her to the mall while the sale is still on." *My hat,* Nini thought, *please don't ask about my new hat.*

"Such a beautiful day," Mim looked up at the pale blue sky. "I think I'll trim the rosemary and rake the rocks in front while it's still cool. What are your plans? Did you say something about Juanito's game?"

"Yes, he has a playoff game at noon. I'm going to clean my room and then Grace and I have homework to finish." Nini's phone dinged. "I think I'll get more bacon. Can I refill your coffee?" she asked as she disappeared through the back door.

She's so responsible, Mim thought, *she babysits, makes breakfast. Maybe I should have let her go to the park last night.*

Nini returned with Mim's coffee. "I'm going to clean my room and finish my homework."

"Where's your bacon?" Mim's eyebrows knit together. "I thought you were doing homework with Grace."

"I'm full," she rubbed her stomach, "and Grace finished her homework already. They'll pick me up on their way to the game."

Mim was puzzled, but said, "I'm going to walk later. Want to join me?"

"Maybe." Nini kissed her mom's cheek and turned toward the back door thinking, *Oh Mom, I really messed up. I should have listened to you. Grace is mad because I went to the party. The older girls mocked me. Ruben caught Luis kissing me and made me come home. I hate high school, I hate everyone.*

Mim was putting the rake in the garage when the Vegas pulled into the driveway. Hortensia waved from the driver's seat. Her husband, Juan, sat beside her, refusing to be seen behind the wheel of a woman's car.

Nini came through the garage door, “Mom, I like the yellow top.” She kissed Mim, then climbed into the crowded minivan. Mim waved as they backed out, chuckling as the machismo facade of Grace’s father crumbled with his toothy grin, a trophy from his days as a soccer star. Wiping the sweat from her forehead, she retreated into the house.

Mim poured a jumbo glass of lemonade and went to her room where she relaxed into the high-back chair by the patio door. She sighed as she pulled up the text she had sent Rod last night. “Nini and I found some great sales at the mall today. How’d your day go?”

“Long day of baseball. Can’t wait to get the boys in bed.”

The boys, the boys, Mim thought, *always the boys. If it weren’t for the boys. Stop,* she scolded herself.

Her art portfolio was propped against the closet door. The drawing of the soaring eagle. She recalled the wounded look on Rod’s face when he realized she had ripped the totem that once bound them together.

I’ll repair it and surprise him, Mim thought. She gathered her drawing tools, retrieved the picture, and went to the living room where she put on some relaxing piano music, and set to work.

The distant sound of her phone disrupted her concentration. It was a text from Nini. “Game over. Going to celebrate the victory. Home later, OK?”

“Game over.” Mim stepped back to look at the drawing she had been working on. She had bandaged the gash on the back so it was hardly noticeable and camouflaged the wound in the rock from which the eagle soared with strategic shading. A tall pine in the background drew attention away from the scar. Yes, the image was restored. A calming peace settled over her.

She took several deep breaths. A soft scent of marshmallow. She glanced at the wooden cabinet in its place of honor by the window, expecting to see a glow emanating from the sunbaked urn enshrined within. Rosie, she thought, I miss your marshmallowy smell. Gooey, playful, comforting, addicting.

Inhaling again, she was filled with a strange knowing. She clutched the drawing to her, then flipped it over and wrote:

Again the paths of the soaring eagles

Converge, intertwine

In ecstasy they rise ever higher

Together

Toward their destiny

Mim was buoyed by her afternoon of drawing. She bobbed along the Loop Trail, pebbles shushing beneath her feet. She had direction. *It's time,* she thought, *time to bring my family back together.* The late afternoon sun warmed on her face. She looked up. High overhead an eagle suspended in the air. A sign. She was overcome with a feeling of urgency.

A loud bark startled her as an oversized German shepherd bounded up the trail. "Bandit?" He sniffed at her and danced about. She held out her hand. "Do you remember me?" She leaned over for a sloppy kiss and scratched behind his ears. "What are you doing out here?" He barked again and turned. She followed him around the bend. There was Joseph at the picnic site.

"Look who I found," she said. "What are you two doing out here? Not working, I hope."

"You're looking ebullient today." He hugged her, then stepped back. "I like the top."

"Thank you. Nini and I went shopping yesterday."

Joseph wedged a can into the overflowing trash bin. "Somebody had quite a party out here last night."

Mim shook her head. "And left a mess for you to clean up. Who would do that?"

"From the gifts they left behind, I'd say some of our high school students." He held open a plastic grocery sack. A flipflop, a Willow Springs High School t-shirt, and a dusty pink cap. Mim's mouth fell open.

"What is it?" Joseph said.

"Can I just see?" Mim reached for the bag. Nini's new hat.

"Mim?"

She shook her head from side to side. "My responsible daughter."

"Nini?"

"I told her I didn't want her out here. I thought she was with Grace. She sat right there at breakfast this morning and told me all about babysitting last night."

“Don’t jump to conclusions, Mim. Give her a chance to explain.”

“Thanks for your advice, Professor. She lied to me.”

Joseph scanned the horizon of soft pinks bleeding to magenta and deep purple. “Look at that sunset. We’d better go before it gets dark.”

Mim was silent on the ride back to the Education Center. Joseph pulled up next to her car. He put a hand on her arm and nodded at the pink cap. “High school can be tough. Trying to fit in.” Mim huffed. “Be patient.”

“Oh, when did you become the expert?” She grabbed the door handle. He leaned closer and kissed her cheek. She got out of the truck, shutting the door harder than she had intended. He waited until she started her car and backed out. The headlights of the last truck in the lot came on. Joseph drove away.

Joseph stopped by the Freemans for a late Sunday afternoon visit. He knocked, opened the front door, and called out to Bob.

“Joseph,” Bob extended his hand in welcome. “You just missed Addy.”

Joseph smiled. “I came to talk to you. I ran into Mim Rodriguez at the park this afternoon.”

“Harrumph,” Bob cleared his throat. Or was that disapproval?

"Some high school kids had quite a party out there last night and it looks like her daughter was there against her wishes."

"Kids are going to test the waters. It's part of growing up."

"It can be hard, especially going it alone. If she'd stop being so stubborn and marry her ex."

Bob looked at Joseph. "If she'd stop being stubborn..."

Joseph held up his hands in surrender. "I know. But it's different for Addy and me. I couldn't bear being the one to destroy any possibility of Addy and her mother having a relationship. As strained as it has been for the last twenty-five years, who knows what Nancy might do if we were to marry. She is ruthless."

"You don't have to tell me. She does everything she can to make our lives miserable. She'll never change. By the way, I had a visit from someone else who's caused a lot of drama in my family."

"I saw Frank's truck here Friday. Glad he came to see you."

Bob looked like a little boy with a secret. "Maybe not he."

Joseph smirked. "My mother was here? She's pretty clever driving Frank's truck."

"Your mother, my Silver Feather. A visit from her puts a smile on my face."

Mim berated herself all the way home. She was relieved that the house was dark, to have some time alone. She poured a glass of wine and nestled into the leather chair in the living room. Her thoughts swirled. *Nini went to the party. That's why she was acting strange this morning. How did I not see it? Joseph said high school is tough, give her a chance.*

The heavy front door opened and Nini burst into the living room. "How was your afternoon, Mom? Did you have a nice time at the park with Joseph? Why didn't you tell me he was back?"

Mim reeled, "You might have seen him yourself had you gone back to get your hat," she pointed to the pink cap on the coffee table.

"It was an innocent party," Nini rolled her eyes, "not like your affair with Joseph. I bet he liked that yellow top." She poked her finger at her mother. "Is that why you've been so happy? I thought it was because of Dad!" Her eyes bore into her mother's as she donned her cap. "You are a liar. I hate you."

Mim stared in stunned disbelief. The tromping of Nini's footsteps down the hall was punctuated by the deliberate locking of her bedroom door. She held her hand to her chest, her heart thumping. *"Give her a chance," Joseph had said. What about giving me a chance?* Mim thought. She clenched her fists, too angry to talk to her daughter and too numb to cry. She stared out the window into the darkness.

Inside her room, Nini flung the hat at the closet door, hitting it with a satisfying "thwap." She fell onto her bed, reliving the nightmare of last night. She was flattered when Luis grabbed her hat off her head and teased her. But then the older girls stepped in. They had circled around her, taunting her. Ali rescued her and ditched the hat under a bush. "You're all over it with the top," she had said. Luis must have agreed. He had kissed her and was just inching his hand under her shirt when Ruben showed up. Her protector. He was so mad, he punched Luis, escorted her to his truck, and brought her home. How could he?

And tonight, when she was about to head home, having kept a safe distance from him all day, he pulled into the driveway.

"Hey, Nini Banini, guess who I saw making out with Joseph Begay in his truck at the park?" Nini had no interest in Joseph Begay nor in whom he was kissing. "C'mon. Short woman? Wavy hair? Might have been your mom?"

"You're making that up."

"Sure looked like her. Sexy yellow top?" He cocked his head. "Guess guys can't keep their hands off you Rodriguez girls." Nini felt like she'd been punched in the gut. He placed a comforting hand on her shoulder. "Hey, I'm just messing with you," he said.

Light shone under her door. *Mom?* She watched. A shadow. *Mom?* It disappeared. Nini curled up on her bed and reached for the picture of Rosie watching over her from the nightstand. "Rosie," tears streamed down her cheeks, "I wish I were with you."

7

MIM WAS UP AT FIRST LIGHT and got ready for the day. She took her coffee to the patio. The morning was still chilly, but she left the back door open. She heard Nini in the kitchen, opening a cupboard, closing the refrigerator. *This is silly*, Mim thought. "Nini," she called, entering the kitchen as the front door closed. She peered out the window and watched her daughter get into the truck, willing her to turn around. "I love you," she said.

Nini stared out the passenger window. Ruben whined, "I can't believe I have a math test this morning. On a Monday, like we're supposed to spend the weekend studying."

"I know," Grace said, "we shouldn't have homework on weekends, although I had time to read my history while I was babysitting Saturday night." She looked at Nini and smirked, "Did you get yours done?"

I don't need this right now, Nini thought, but said, "My reading? Yeah, I did it when my mom and I got home from the mall." *Where I bought that stupid pink hat and my mom bought that top she wore on her walk with Joseph.* She placed her right hand on the long sleeve that covered her left arm.

When they arrived at school, Ruben joined his soccer buddies in the parking lot. Nini and Grace headed to the freshman hallway.

"I'll put my stuff away and meet you at your locker," Grace said.

"You don't have to. I can meet you in class," Nini walked ahead.

Grace pulled on Nini's backpack. "Hey, I'm sorry I got mad at you. I was jealous that I got stuck babysitting. I'll get my stuff and be right back."

Nini shuffled through the crowd to her locker. As she reached up to retrieve her biology book, she heard Grace's voice.

"Nini," she grimaced at the oozing cuts on Nini's arm. "C'mon, let's find the counselor."

"No," Nini shook her head, eyes pleading.

What happened to you? Grace wondered. "Maybe later?"

Nini pulled the sleeve down. "Let's get to class. We'll be late."

Nini saw Ms. Linstrom speaking but she didn't hear a word. The cuts on her arm burned. Her thoughts swirled. *Mom was making out with Joseph. Ruben caught me kissing Luis. I'm a slut just like my mother.*

Grace glanced back at Nini. *This is my fault*, she thought. *I need to tell someone, but if I leave, Nini will know. I'll find Ruben after class. He'll know what to do.*

When the bell rang, Grace waited for Nini. "I have to stop by my locker," she lied. "You go on and I'll meet you at lunch."

She maneuvered through the noisy passageway toward the front office. She spotted Ruben and waved.

"Are you lost? This is upperclassmen territory."

"Ruben, it's Nini. She cut." Grace made slicing motions across her forearm.

"Nini? Cut?" He shook his head, "she'd never do that."

"I saw it this morning. All red and swollen. What should we do?"

"Let me think about it. I'll catch you after lunch." *This is my fault,* he thought. *I should've watched out for her at the party.*

Ruben hurried to the cafeteria after PE. Grace and Nini were laughing as they came down the hall. *Nini looks like she's in a good mood. I'll wait to see what happens,* Ruben thought. He noticed Grace raise her eyebrows and shrug her shoulders.

"Hey Graciela, Nini Banini," he said as Luis fell into step beside him. He winked, his eye puffy and purple.

"Meet me at the truck after school," Ruben said, "and I'll take you home before soccer practice."

Ruben was sitting in the truck when Grace and Nini showed up. Nini climbed in next to him. "How did everything go today?" he said.

She averted her eyes and rested her hand on her sleeve. *He knows,* she thought.

"Let me take you home and we can talk to your mom."

Tears pooled in Nini's eyes. She held her hand up. "No. I don't want to talk to her."

"Hey," Ruben said, "I'm sorry I talked you into going to the party with me."

"And I'm sorry I got mad at you for going without me," Grace added.

Nini looked from one to the other. "You think...?"

"We're worried about you," Ruben said. "Come home with us then." Ruben turned down Laguna Street.

Hortensia was waiting for them at the front door. She kissed Ruben and Grace and wrapped her arms around Nini, who began to cry. "Oh now, tell me what happened." As they passed through the kitchen, she nodded at the pitcher on the counter. "Grace, bring the iced tea."

They gathered in their usual places around the patio table. Grace told her mother about the cuts she had seen on Nini's arm.

"Cuts? Does she need stitches?"

"No Mama, it's like, sometimes kids cut," she made slicing motions on her arm with her fingers, "when they are scared or hurt." Nini pulled back the sleeve of her black shirt, revealing the swollen red scratches.

"Oh Nini, why would you do that?" Hortensia said.

"It's my fault," Ruben looked down. "I took her to the party with me on Saturday."

"And I got mad because she left me," Grace said.

Hortensia frowned. “You went with Ruben? I thought you were babysitting.”

“I’m sorry, but, it’s not you,” she said to Ruben and Grace. “It’s my mom. She was making out with Joseph Begay at the park.”

Hortensia was shocked. “When? How do you know that?”

“Yesterday. Ruben saw them when he went to get his jacket.”

“Are you sure?” Hortensia looked at Ruben, then turned to Nini, “What did your mother say? Has she seen the cuts?”

“She’s just going to lie. She doesn’t care.”

“She’s your mother. You need to tell her.”

“I don’t want anything to do with her.”

“Then I’m going to tell her,” Hortensia said. She left them sitting at the table.

Hortensia steered out of their cul de sac toward Mim’s house three blocks away. She passed the park and recalled their first meeting there thirteen years ago when Mim and Nini moved into the neighborhood. She had introduced herself when she saw how well their little girls played together. She remembered consoling Mim on that bench when Rod married Eva. Mim had been certain they would get back together. She pulled into Mim’s driveway, having avoided thoughts of her mission. What would she say to her dear friend? She lowered her head as she walked to the door and rang the bell.

Mim turned down the taco meat cooking on the stove and met Hortensia at the door. “Come in,” Mim embraced her. “Have you seen Nini? I thought she’d be home by now.”

“She’s at our house,” she said in a soft voice. “Grace and Ruben brought her home.” She paused. “They didn’t know what else to do.”

“What do you mean ‘what else to do’?”

Hortensia looked at Mim. *How do I tell her?* she wondered.

“Hortensia?” Mim was getting anxious. “What happened to Nini?”

“She cut herself,” she said, slicing her hand across her arm as Grace had done.

“Cut herself?” Mim repeated, unsure she heard correctly. She took Hortensia’s arm to steady herself. “Why didn’t someone call me? Why didn’t you bring her home?”

Hortensia stared down at the tile, “She didn’t want to come home. She thinks you betrayed her.”

A door slammed in the driveway. Nini? Mim opened the door.

Rod, all business in a navy blue suit, tucked his sunglasses in the jacket pocket, then slicked his hair back, as he strode toward her.

“Rod, I’m so glad...” Mim began.

“When were you,” he stopped when he saw Hortensia. “I need to speak with Mim and Nini in private.”

"Nini's not here," Mim said, her voice empty. "She's at the Vegas."

"Maybe that's for the best," Rod said. "Hortensia, my apologies."

"I was just leaving." She glanced at Mim in silent support and closed the door in a hush behind her.

"Why didn't you tell me Begay's back?" Rod searched Mim's eyes.

"I just found out myself," she said.

"And I heard you were thrilled to see him."

"What are you talking about?" Mim tilted her head.

"You don't have to play innocent. Nini called me."

Mim's eyebrows knit together, "When?"

"Last night. Sobbing. How could you do this?"

Mim reached out to him. "Come in and let me explain."

Rod held up his hand. "I don't need an explanation."

The front door opened and Nini walked in, startling Rod and Mim. Ruben, broad and muscular, stood behind her like a warrior, a shock of shaggy black hair falling over his forehead.

"Dad," Nini hugged Rod and looked at her mother, defiance masking her guilt.

"Ruben," Mim said, "thanks for bringing Nini home. I think we'll be fine now."

"Yes," Rod agreed and held the door open. "We have some talking to do."

"No," Nini stepped between Ruben and Rod. "I want him to stay."

"I don't see why..." Mim said.

Rod interrupted her. "Okay then. Why don't we all go into the living room?"

The blinds of the sunken living room were drawn against the afternoon sun. Ruben sat beside Nini on the sofa, pulling at the edges of his soccer shorts. Rod took the chair beside Nini and motioned for Mim to take the chair opposite him. She remained standing and nodded at Nini. "Let's see your arm."

Rod was confused. *Her arm?*

Nini raised her shirtsleeve, her jaw tensed with pain. Rod and Mim stared, unprepared for what they saw: five slashes, red, swollen, oozing. They looked at each other, the concern in Mim's eyes pleading, "What do we do?" The fury in Rod's eyes blaming, "Look what you've done."

Rod placed his hand on Nini's shoulder. "Why would you do this?" He nodded at her arm.

Nini lifted the sleeve over the cuts and held her shoulders back. "You didn't tell him, Mom?" Her eyes burned into her mother's. "Ruben saw her making out with Joseph at the park."

Mim glared at Ruben, her eyes wide with shock.

Ruben stared at his feet, stretched out beside Nini's under the coffee table. He felt Mim's eyes on him and looked at her. "I saw you in Mr. Begay's truck yesterday." He rubbed his hands up and down his silky shorts; he was backed into a corner. He leaned toward Nini. "I, I was just messing with you," his deep voice apologized. "I never thought you'd..." He pointed at her arm. "I'm so sorry." He looked at Nini, then Rod and Mim.

"And are you sorry you took her to that party Saturday night?" Mim said. "The one I told her she couldn't go to." She looked at Nini. Ruben flinched.

"It was my idea," Nini stared back at her. "I made him take me." *Because I hoped Luis would be there*, she thought.

"It wasn't a big deal," Ruben said, "just some kids hanging out. I'm sorry. I should've known better."

Rod thought back to the fun he had with his high school buddies at the Tastee Freez on the edge of town. "You need to start using your head." He tapped the side of Ruben's cap, then offered his hand and ushered him to the door.

When Rod returned, Mim and Nini sat staring at each other, the anger between them palpable. He took Ruben's place on the couch beside Nini and put his arm around her. "Talk to us, Mija. We love you so much," he said. "What can we do?"

Nini jerked her head toward Mim, "She's already done enough."

"If you'd just let me speak," Mim said, her voice firm.

Rod held up his hand, his head still bent toward their daughter. "Would it help to see a counselor?" he said.

"Obviously I don't know what I'm doing," Mim threw her arms in the air, then lowered her voice, "maybe talking to a counselor would help."

"I don't need therapy," Nini rolled her eyes. "I'm fine."

"Fine?" Mim said, "you accuse me of making out with Joseph. You cut yourself. You call that fine?" She clutched the arms of the chair, eyes wide. *Rod, talk to her.*

He rubbed Nini's back. "Let your mom and me talk about this," his look warned Mim not to object, "then we'll decide together what's best for our family."

Nini harrumphed. She stood and folded her arms across her chest. "Can I go now?"

"Yes," Rod kissed her cheek. "Mim, why don't you walk me out?"

The front door closed and Nini heard her mom's voice, "Like it or not, she needs to see a counselor."

I do not need a counselor, Nini thought. She opened the garage door to a blast of hot air. A basket of laundry sat atop the washing machine. There was just enough light for her to maneuver between her mom's SUV and the tools that hung on the wall. "Ouch," she caught the rake she had stepped on with one hand and covered her mouth with the other. She listened. Had they heard her?

"... see someone, too."

"Me? I didn't cut," Mim said.

"You said there's more to it than that. She went to a party?"

"She lied to me."

"Maybe you should have let her go," Rod said. "After all, she is in high school now."

"I know, but I'm afraid. If something happens to her."

"We can do this together," Rod said. "We owe it to Nini and to us."

"Now's not a good time."

Rod's voice was soft. Nini leaned closer. "Now may be the best time. The nightmares are back. You brought out the portfolio for a reason. Show her the drawing. Tell her the truth."

The truth? Nini's cuts burned.

"I can't, Rod. She'll hate me."

"She won't hate you. She'll understand. I promise."

There was a long silence, then Mim's muffled voice, "Can we start with the counselor? I think that's more important right now."

Nini gritted her teeth. *I do not need a counselor.*

"Okay," Rod said, his voice flat. "Let's ask around. See who might be good for her." Nini's shoulders sagged. "And for you too."

"Don't put this on me, Rod," Mim said, "I don't need a counselor. And I'll decide when to tell her."

Tell me what? Nini wanted to scream.

"Mim," Rod said.

"Good night."

Nini heard the truck door close. She dashed past the tools, knocking a hoe off its hook, and opened the door a crack.

Mmm, the aroma of taco meat wafted from the kitchen. *I could wait and ask her, but then she'd know I was listening.* Holding her growling stomach, Nini scampered down the hall, reaching her room as the front door opened.

Rod rested his head against the steering wheel, defeated. After a moment, he took a deep breath and backed out of the driveway. He put the truck in gear and headed east, so lost in his thoughts that he missed the lone eagle, wings outstretched, floating on the air current above the desert.

Mim paused a moment outside the front door. *I wish I could rewind my afternoon,* she thought. *I wish it could be Nini and me fixing dinner in the kitchen like we always do. Maybe Rod is right. Maybe now is the time. Should I tell her? Maybe she'll be eating dinner. Maybe she'll be waiting in the living room. Then, I can tell her.* "Tell her, tell her," Rod's voice echoed in her head.

She opened the door to a dark foyer. The smell of the taco meat to be shared with her daughter reminded her of the rift between them. *Tell her.*

A glimmer of light under Nini's door beckoned. *Tell her.* Mim stopped. *Tell her.* "Are you ready to hear the truth?" Mim muttered to the door. *Am I strong enough to tell you and risk losing you too?* she wondered. She dragged down the hallway to her room.

Mim lay in her bed in her nightshirt and massaged the searing pain of her right wrist. The scars from the cuts had long since healed, but the memory was vivid.

Fourteen years ago. Chaco State Park. Mim was perched on the edge of the concrete bench. She took a deep breath, tasting the tar smell of the creosote that dotted the desert around them. The sun shone in the soft blue New Mexico sky flecked with dove gray clouds.

Three year old Rosie crouched by a rain-filled rivulet that ran along the edge of the picnic area and disappeared into the desert landscape. She jabbed a stick into the mud and peeked up, with the dark mischievous eyes of her father.

She's such a good girl. Mim looked at the backpack on the cement picnic table. *She's playing. She'll be fine.* She removed the sketch pad and took up her pencil. She felt a pulsing from her heart to her hand. The image of Rod flashed in her head. *Do you feel the same thing when you pick up a bat?* she wondered.

"Look Mommy," Rosie cupped a rock in her hand like a precious gem.

"It's beautiful," Mim said, her pencil poised above her sketch pad. "Mommy's going to draw a few minutes while you play."

She looked at Rosie and began to draw the face of the free-spirited child etched into her heart: the brown eyes, the pixie nose above her full mauve lips, the stubborn line of her chin, surrounded by a halo of wavy chestnut hair. Mim looked up, "Rosie?" She panicked. There she was. She had wandered back toward the trail, a fistful of rocks in her hand. “Rosie, c’mon back, Sweetheart. Remember what Daddy said?”

“Be a good girl,” Rosie’s voice sang back, as she moseyed toward the shelter, mud caked on her shoes.

I knew we should have put those boots on, Mim thought. She sketched in the details of the elephant print dress and the dark, wet strip along the bottom. *Oh Rosie.* She caught a glimpse of the navy blue dress and looked up. *Rosie?*

There she was moving up the rivulet poking her stick into the water. “Rosie Rodriguez,” Mim called, walking toward her. Rosie turned. Mim saw the snake in the rocks and froze.

“Rosie,” she whispered, trying not to alarm her daughter, “stay still.” Mim tiptoed closer, hoping to get there before...

The rattlesnake struck; Rosie screamed.

“Rosie,” Mim’s cry caught in her throat.

Mom? Nini woke, lying on her bed, still in her clothes. She listened. *I must’ve been dreaming,* she thought.

The house was quiet.

MIM SPOTTED SILKIE'S BRIGHT orange jeep before she pulled into the Education Center parking lot. Silkie loved that jeep and the warm weather. She scooted around town with the top off, teasing she was "going topless."

Sporting her peach Fit Fanny tee, her friend was doing squats near the trail. Mim had not been surprised by Silkie's text this morning, "Walk with me after work?" *She knows.* Mim's initial irritation turned to gratitude. *Silkie always knows.*

Mim grabbed her cap and water bottle and joined her friend to warm up before heading up Black Hawk Trail. A map on the wooden sign at the head of the trail outlined the two-mile loop to Black Hawk Lake. *Where Joseph taught Nini to fish,* Mim thought. She could still see the three of them, Joseph, carrying the tackle box and poles, four year old Nini, skipping along beside him, and Bandit lumbering behind.

Mim and Silkie hiked the slight incline that led to the lake. It was dusty. There had been no rain in several weeks. The grasses were brittle. They walked a ways before Mim broke the silence. "You know Nini cut herself." She choked on the words and took a moment to recover. "You taught kids for a long time. Did you ever have anyone cut?"

The faces of troubled students scrolled through Silkie's mind. "More than I like to remember. From one-timers to self-mutilators."

The bright red scratches on Nini's soft flesh were vivid in Mim's mind. "Rod blames me," she said. "Ruben told Nini he saw me making out with Joseph."

Silkie waited. She didn't believe it, though she recalled Mim's scare over a decade ago after a weekend with Joseph in the canyon.

"Rod and I confronted him last night and he said he was just teasing. But I don't think they believed him."

"And poor Ruben, look what it did to Nini," Silkie said. "I'm surprised though. I always thought she loved Joseph."

"I don't know why she dislikes him so."

"Jealous maybe?" Silkie said.

"Of Joseph? He's old enough to be her grandfather."

Silkie looked at Mim, feigning offense. At fifty-eight, she was four years older than Joseph.

"Not that old, but you know what I mean," Mim said. "Even so, is that so devastating that she'd cut herself?"

"At that age, you might be surprised."

"I tried to tell Rod I think it's more than that. She went to a party Saturday night when I told her she couldn't go."

"What'd Rod say?"

"He blamed me for that, too. He said I should have trusted her, I should have let her go. I feel like a terrible mother. I don't know what to do," Mim said.

"What do you want to do?"

Silkie always said that. "What do I want to do?" Mim paused. "I want to go home and hold her. Tell her how sad I am that I wasn't there for her and she cut. I want her to know how much I love her."

They continued around the winding path in contemplative silence, the sun warming their faces. Mim's footsteps echoed Rod's voice, "Tell her, tell her." She looked out at the desert landscape, the azure sky, and the mountains, strong and tall.

Just before they reached the parking lot, Mim said, "Silkie, you know Nini. Do you think it would help her to talk to a counselor?"

"I do," she said. "I think it would help if you both did."

Nini closed the heavy front door, relieved to be home. All day she felt like she was being watched. Grace was at her side like a puppy. Ruben appeared between classes. Even Mr. Mercer wished her a good afternoon on her way out of school.

She thought about seeing Luis after lunch. His dark eyes twinkled beneath lady-killer lashes, the bruise almost gone now. His smile made her day. Behind him came Ali with that monstrous basketball-player boyfriend. Ali grinned and gave her a thumbs-up.

Nini's stomach growled. She wandered into the kitchen for a snack. A note from her mom on the counter lay beside a can of beans and a box of rice: "Going for a walk with Silkie. Leftovers tonight?" A squiggled heart, "Mom." *I'll start the rice after I change my shirt,* Nini thought.

Heading to her room, she spied the portfolio resting against her mom's closet and thought of the picture of her and Bandit. *I wish I could wrap my arms around his furry neck,* she thought and smiled, remembering his slobbery kisses on her cheeks.

She slipped into the room, opened the folder, and flipped through the drawings. *Here it is.* There was Joseph in his park ranger uniform behind the wheel of his old truck; Bandit in the middle, his tongue lolling out the side of his mouth; and her three year old self, head barely visible above the dashboard, her arm flung over Bandit's neck. "Look at us," she said, "you and me and Joseph." She shook her head. *No, not Joseph.* With a stab of guilt, she jammed the drawing into the folder behind a crumpled page.

She plucked it from the portfolio. *What is this?* An unfinished drawing smudged with dirt. A little girl crouched down, her thick wavy hair like a mane surrounding her impish face. "Hi Rosie. What are you doing in here?" There she was, stick in hand, mischief in her eyes. "Dad always says you were the precocious one," Nini said. Something nagged at her. Her dad's voice, "Show her the drawing."

"Nini, what are you doing in here?" Mim stood in the doorway, her eyes wide.

Nini looked at her mother. "Dad said, 'Tell her about the drawing.'" She shoved the picture at her mother and said, "Is this the drawing, Mom?"

"You found it," Mim said, overwhelmed by every thought, every feeling, every fear, she ever had about the moment Nini found out the truth. "She'll understand," Rod's voice urged. *She'll never understand,* Mim thought. She had no feeling left. She was a cardboard image of herself. She stared at the drawing in Nini's hand.

"I was exhausted. Teaching all week, taking care of your dad after his injury, and you girls," she said, her voice a monotone. "The rain had finally stopped. I wanted to go on a hike by myself, but your dad insisted I take Rosie. And she was an angel, skipping ahead of me, picking up rocks. We stopped at a picnic area," Mim paused. "I hoped a picture of Rosie playing would lift your dad's spirits. I got so absorbed in the drawing, I never thought, a rattler? When I looked up, she was gone. I raced to her at the edge of the clearing and saw the snake and..."

Nini swiped at the tears dripping off her chin, then reared up, "All these years you said it was an accident. You're a liar." Her eyes bored into her mother's, "I wish it had been you."

MIM SLUMPED INTO THE cushioned chair on the patio and let her head flop back, too tired to hold it up. She had spent all of her energy pretending to be her cheery self at the coffee shop, going through the motions, feeling nothing.

"Tell her the truth," Rod had said. "I promise things will be better." *You were wrong about that, weren't you, Rod?* Mim thought. *Nini may never speak to me...*

The patio door creaked open. "Nini," Mim stood to greet her. "I was just thinking of you. I'm so glad..."

Nini looked at her mother, trepidation in her gray eyes. Rod stood behind her.

"I guess I shouldn't be surprised to see you," Mim said, "though it is a bit early." She glanced at her watch.

Nini took the chair across from her mother and Rod sat at the end of the table. "I picked her up after lunch," he nodded at Nini. "Tom Mercer called me."

"Tom called you?" Mim said. Nini stared down at her hands.

"She was in the nurse's office, couldn't stop crying. You should have called me last night."

Mim looked at him, drained of all feeling. *Call you?* she thought, *to let you know I trusted you? And you were wrong?*

"Nini and I talked." He put his hand on Nini's arm. "She's had a tough couple of weeks with school starting, hearing about you and..."

Me and? Mim's eyes grew wide. *Say it Rod, Joseph. Me and Joseph. I did nothing wrong.* Her voice was loud in her head. She stared at him. *This is the man who proclaimed his love for me?*

"Her cutting, and," Rod looked into Mim's eyes, trying his best to relay this last part with the love he felt for her. "finding out that..."

Nini sat up. "You lied. It was no accident, it was your fault," she pointed at Mim. "You and your precious drawing. 'It was the perfect day,' you said. 'I wanted to show your dad.' Well you sure did, didn't you? You were so busy, you let my sister wander right into the path of that snake."

"Nini," Rod said.

"It's okay," Mim said. "I've denied the truth all these years. I was afraid you wouldn't love me, afraid I would lose you too."

Nini glanced at Rod.

"What?" Mim said.

Rod ran his hand over his hair, "Nini and I talked this afternoon." He looked at Nini. Do you want to change your mind? his eyes asked. Nini looked away.

Mim stiffened, her defenses on alert.

"We think she needs a little time away, time to process all of this."

"Okay," Mim said. "Maybe she could spend some time with you."

"Not with Dad," Nini scoffed.

"Uh," Rod looked at Mim, "I talked to Hortensia and she said Nini can stay with them for a week or so."

Mim's mind was spinning. *Nini needs space. You talked to Hortensia?* She looked at Rod like he was some alien creature.

"We decided she could move on Friday."

"You decided?" Mim stood, knocking over the chair, "you and Hortensia?" She crossed her arms and faced Nini. "You need some time and space to think? You can have your space. And you don't have to wait until Friday." Mim walked to the door. "You can go now. Go ahead. Pack your things and go now." The door stuttered shut behind her.

Stunned, Rod looked at Nini. "She doesn't mean it, give me a minute to talk to her."

"No," Nini's chair screeched against the tile. "Mom wants me gone? Give me ten minutes and I'll be ready."

Rod stared out at the wispy clouds gathering above the mountains in the east and shook his head. His heart lay in a puddle in his chest. *All I wanted was to give them a chance to think things through. I'll talk to Mim, help her see I mean well.*

He heard Nini bustling behind her door as he went down the hall. He knocked on Mim's door. "Mim? Let me in, please.

I just want to talk to you." He waited. *Please, let me tell you it will be okay. Let me hold you. I love you so much.*

Nini's door opened. "Dad, I'm ready."

Rod was shocked when he looked in the room. The walls were bare. Even the bedspread and sheets were gone. She handed him a large box and retrieved her suitcase. Without a glance toward her mother's room, she lowered her head and walked down the hall.

Mim sat against her bed, knees pulled to her chest, her heart pounding. *What have I done?*

"... talk to you."

She lifted her head. *Rod? Rod, wait one minute.* She wiped the tears from her cheeks, fluffed her hair with her fingers, and stood. She went to the door. "Rod," she said. The hall was empty. The front door shut.

10

MIM STEPPED INTO THE hallway of Cactus Coffee and closed the door on the black and white world she inhabited since Nini left. The aroma of coffee beans infused her with a false sense of normalcy. The sign on the Fit Fanny door, "No classes Saturday."

She unlocked the door to her shop. The morning sun cast a shimmering image of the stained glass cactus onto the tile floor.

Mim busied herself with her morning routine: putting coffee on to brew, placing pastries in the display case, playing some upbeat music. She caught herself humming as she slid the mugs from the drying rack into the cubbies on the back wall.

She swept the front sidewalk, watered the planters of red geraniums and spiky fountain grass, and plucked a few dry leaves from the foliage that cascaded over the side. At seven o'clock she flipped the sign on the front window to "OPEN."

An older couple who had been waiting in their car joined her inside. They were the only people in the shop for a long hour when a young man with longish blond hair hanging out the back of his UNM cap showed up. He selected a LOBOS mug from the shelf for his morning brew and made his way to the booth by the front window. He opened his laptop and slid his headphones on.

At midmorning, Mim was relieved to hear the bells chime as Silkie and Tom entered the shop with Wes and Marie Robbins. She grabbed the dish detergent and ran some hot water into the counter sink.

“Hi, Mim,” Silkie said.

“I missed you this morning. I hope you’re enjoying your day off.”

Mim looked up at the imposing figure beside her. "Tom,” she nodded, thinking, *Traitor, why did you call Rod instead of me the other day?*

“Good morning, Mim,” he said. He looked at her with gentle green eyes. “Sorry about the incident with Nini on Wednesday.” Mim dropped a cup into the soapy water. “I’m sad to hear she moved out.” *Thanks for not saying that I threw her out,* Mim thought. “You know I am here for all of you.”

She dried her hands. “What can I get you this morning?”

Silkie placed two mugs on the counter. She gave Mim the black one with “Willow Springs Stallions“ in gold block letters. “Dark roast for Tom,” she said, “and for me,” she handed her a white mug with a red heart on it, “white chocolate mocha,” they said together.

“Wes, Marie, what are you up to this morning?” They were both tall and fit for being in their late fifties. Marie’s white hair was cut in a stylish bob. She teased that the hair was from more than four decades as the high school French teacher.

"We're having coffee with Tom and Silkie," Wes said, wrapping his arm around his wife's shoulder, "before we head out to the golf course." Wes was a topnotch golfer.

"I didn't know you golfed, Marie," Mim said.

"I've had a few lessons over the years," she chuckled, "but I'm not very good." Her blue eyes twinkled.

"She's good with the golf cart," Wes winked at Marie. "We like to get out and spend time together."

Mim poured their coffee. "Here you go. I'll bring your pastries right over." She took a tray from beneath the counter.

"Wes, you take the coffee," Marie said. "I'll be right there."

Mim put a couple of blueberry scones and banana bars on the tray. She handed it to Marie.

"Thanks," Marie said. She tucked a note into Mim's hand.

Mim slid the paper into the back pocket, curious about its contents. She glanced around the shop. The young man in the front booth stared out the window. Mim followed his gaze to the Square across the street.

A teenager threw a Frisbee for his dog. Two couples chatted together by the sandbox watching their children play. An old man in a floppy hat slouched on a bench by the gazebo. He sat up when a girl from the florist shop stopped by and spoke to him. He nodded at the large box in her hands. She pointed toward Cactus Coffee. The boy playing Frisbee gawked as she passed. The dog barked and ran over. She patted it on the head, then strolled across the Square to the shop, her red ponytail swinging in time to her steps.

The chimes rang as she pushed the front door open with her shoulder. She waltzed to the counter and handed a card to Mim. Everyone watched. Mim could almost hear them saying, “Who is it from? Open the card.”

Marie mouthed, “Rod?” to Silkie who shrugged and frowned.

Mim had not heard from Nini or Rod since Wednesday. *Why would he send flowers today? To the coffee shop?* She peeked into the box at a fall wreath of yellow and orange zinnias dotted with berry sprigs and oak leaves. She opened the card, confirmed it was from Rod, and slipped it into her pocket. She closed the lid of the box and put it out of sight in the back room.

The student chatted with the delivery girl, his headphones around his neck. Tom, Wes, Silkie, and Marie pushed their chairs in. Tom and Wes waved as they headed to the door, while Silkie and Marie brought the cups and plates to the dish bin by the counter.

Marie patted Mim’s arm, “See you Monday.”

Silkie hugged her. “I’m here if you need me,” she whispered and slipped out the door behind the delivery girl.

Mim reached into her pocket for the note from Marie. “Mim, Maureen has been a savior to me. She might be able to help you too. Marie.” There was a business card inside.

Maureen Sherman, LMFC. *Marie went to a marriage and family counselor?* Mim wrapped the note around the business card and returned it to her pocket. She would call Maureen first thing Monday morning.

She fingered the card from Rod. She hesitated, took it from her pocket and read, "Mim, this fall wreath is a symbol of our unending love. We will make it through this together, Rod."

Yeah, she thought, *isn't fall when life as we know it comes to an end?*

"A secret admirer?" The college student stood at the front door, adjusting his backpack. "The card," he said.

"Yes, I suppose," she smirked.

Mim was getting milk from the back fridge when she heard the chimes clink again. "Did you forget...?" Mim recognized the silhouette in the door. Joseph.

Of course, she thought. *Tom and Silkie show up. Marie gives me the name of a therapist. Rod sends flowers.* "What brings you out today?"

"Mim," he met her in the middle of the empty shop and grasped her hand. "I was in town visiting some folks at the nursing home. I stopped by to see if you're busy tonight." Mim eyed him. "We haven't had a chance to catch up since I've been back. Would you join me for the Night Sky Event at the park this evening?"

"Night Sky Event?" She looked at the bulletin board on the wall. "I didn't know there was an event at the park tonight."

He smiled, mischief in his eyes. “There will be if you join me. Pick you up at seven?”

With a look of gratitude, Mim nodded.

Mim sipped an icy margarita as she dressed for the Night Sky Event. She studied her closet full of clothes, deciding on a pair of tangerine-colored capris, the white tank that she bought at the mall, and slip-on tennis shoes. At the last minute she grabbed her turquoise jacket, as the desert cooled when the sun went down.

Passing the full-length mirror in the hallway, Mim smiled at her reflection, looking sporty with a dash of sassy. She pictured Nini standing there, giggling and twirling and felt the sadness in her heart. She had not heard from her daughter since she moved out. Relieved to see the lights of Joseph’s truck in the driveway, Mim walked out of the empty house closing the heavy door behind her. She greeted Bandit, smiling down from the back of the truck, with a pat on his furry neck, and climbed into the seat beside Joseph.

They rode the few miles to Soaring Eagle in silence enjoying the descending twilight. “I thought we would take the Mesquite Trail this evening. There’s a flat, open space up a ways, perfect for observing the night sky.”

He parked in the turnoff and gathered the blanket and water he had brought. They hiked a short distance before they came to a clearing surrounded by trees and shrubs. They spread out the padded blanket and sat together gazing at the darkening sky.

Mim reclined into a peaceful trance. She felt Joseph's calloused hand on her arm. "There is pain in your heart," he said.

She was silent for a long moment. "I've lost everything. Rosie died. I let Rod go. Nini thinks I betrayed her. They never let me explain, just decided we needed space."

She sat up. He wiped the tears from her eyes. "Others think they know what is best for us. What do you want?"

"I want to wake up and it will all be over. I want my family back, Rod and Nini and me." She took his hand. "I want to be myself." A shooting star blazed across the sky.

They ambled down the trail toward the truck. "Silkie suggested I see a therapist," Mim said. "I think it might help. This morning Marie recommended a woman in Truth or Consequences. I wasn't surprised she knew I was looking for one, but I was surprised that she had seen somebody." Joseph nodded, not sharing what he knew about Marie.

11

MIM WOKE IN THE early hours of Monday morning, looked about her, and sighed. *It was a dream, a vivid dream.* She was in the canyon where Joseph had taken her after Rod married Eva.

The canyon walls rose from the wide rocky riverbed where only a shallow stream now ran. Joseph had his camera in hand as they hiked along enjoying the solitude.

After a picnic lunch by the water, Joseph ambled up the canyon while Mim reclined on the rocks in the warmth of the April sun. She must have dozed off when she heard footsteps crunching along the rocky path.

"Take your clothes off," he nudged her bare foot with his heavy boot.

Take my clothes off? She was drowsy.

He said, "I'll take mine off too," and he unbuttoned his shirt. Her heart beat faster. "C'mon, Mim," he coaxed, sliding his jeans down exposing the taut fawn-colored flesh beneath.

Mim turned and reached for her zipper. She removed her shorts and panties, her t-shirt and, she hesitated before she undid her bra. She heard a "Click" and looked up. His gaze drifted over her silky body. Holding her eyes with his, he leaned down, kissing her slowly. She reached up to run her fingers through his long black hair; he flinched and caught her right hand in a tight grip.

He was a different man as he lowered her to the blanket; something had come over him. He made love to her almost violently, yet she was not afraid. He struggled for a long time before his body wrenched in release. Then he held her like a cherished gift. “I’ve been waiting for you,” he said. A tear slid down his cheek.

That evening Mim sipped a cup of chamomile tea as she relaxed on the patio. She took the folded paper from her pocket. She had called Dr. Sherman that morning and was pleased to get an appointment on Thursday afternoon. Pleased? Relieved. *Maybe I do need therapy.* Mim rubbed her fingers over her forehead.

Today had been the slowest day ever at the shop. Had everyone in Willow Springs heard that Nini had moved out? Mim’s heart crumpled. She would never understand how this little community worked. Community support, they said. Spreading gossip she called it. Even the Morning Men were quiet today. Benny just looked at her. Ralph had the courage to say he was sorry to hear about Nini.

“Yes,” Mim said. “I threw my daughter out. I threw her out. She needed space. Fine. I gave her space. Her mom is a liar.”

Mim felt a chill. Getting up to retrieve her turquoise jacket, she sighed, remembering she had left it in Joseph’s truck. *I’ll pick it up tomorrow,* she thought as she retired into the quiet house.

12

MIM PERKED UP WHEN Ellen, Marie, and Judith arrived for lunch. "Guess we beat the rush," Judith said, glancing around the near-empty shop.

"Tuesday's our favorite, taco salad," Ellen said.

"We wanted to get together before Marie rushes off to her daughter's again," Judith said.

"I'm helping with the Fall Festival at church. Besides, Wes will be busy with the golf tournament all weekend."

"So, three taco salads?" said Mim.

"And iced tea, please," Judith added.

The ladies took the corner booth by the window. Judith was exasperated with her students in the Vietnam Project. "I have six independent thinkers who couldn't agree on a project for this year."

"Remember the year the kids raised money for the commemorative bench in the Square," Marie motioned out the window. "I didn't realize the number of soldiers from our area that we lost or who went missing," she looked at Judith, "or all of our veterans who served."

"I know, and the pen pals was a great idea, writing letters to our veterans and the veterans in Vietnam," Ellen said with reverence. "That was really meaningful for Chet." Though Chet did not talk about it. She had long ago developed compassion after a painful lesson she had learned in the veteran's hospital where they had met. The night he had cried out in anguish, sweat drenching his body. She tried to move his buddy away from the bed so she could help. He had looked at her with distant eyes and said, "You can't."

So many times over these past decades, she endured the helplessness and pain of exclusion. "You can't." Only those who have trod the same path, only they could.

"Yes, what an impact on the students and the vets," Judith said. "This year the group couldn't come to an agreement. Leonard wanted to raise money for a village."

"Good idea," Marie said.

"Then Tran suggested a shoe drive. Students could donate shoes for kids in Vietnam."

"I like that, too," Marie said.

"Well, Leonard didn't. Ali got excited about Tran's idea and said it could be a shoe project. They could get donations from shoe stores, too."

"I always liked Ali's spunk," Marie said.

"Well, I'm not sure what was going on. Leonard pounded the table and said that was a stupid idea and looked at Emma and Chloe for support." Mim came by with more iced tea.

"He wasn't jealous?" Marie again.

"I don't know. Emma agreed with him, but Chloe," Judith thanked Mim for the tea and said, "you remember Chloe, Mim?"

"The 'Goth' girl?"

"Yes, she's usually quiet but she got quite animated about the shoe idea; a project that involved the school and the community working together. In the end, everyone voted for the shoe project, except poor Leonard."

"Maybe his feelings were hurt," Marie said.

"I told him to get over it," Judith said. "The shoe project it is."

"You've been awfully quiet, Ellen. What do you think?"

"Shoes would be a wonderful gift," Ellen said, "Chet might even know where you could send them."

"That's great. Would you ask him?" Judith said.

"I can't." Marie and Judith waited. Mim moved on to the next table. "It would be better if it came from one of the kids."

That evening after another dinner alone, Mim drove to the park. She was looking forward to a long walk and then planned to pick up her jacket at Joseph's. The desert horizon was striped orange and pink. She hiked the loop passing the turnoff where she and Joseph had enjoyed their Night Sky Event. She trekked on, her thoughts floating into the twilight. She finished her walk and texted Joseph that she was stopping by to get her jacket.

Joseph's adobe house was on the outskirts of town, several miles east of the park. She pulled into the circular driveway past his dusty brown truck in the carport. The yellow New Mexico flag fluttered beside a giant old saguaro planted at the edge of the house.

Bandit sprawled in front of the screen door, mesmerized by the flute music playing inside. He lifted his head in greeting, his black ears perked up, his tail thumped the cement.

"Hi, Bandit. You're turning a little gray there," she rubbed his muzzle.

Joseph appeared at the door, "He's showing his age, isn't he?"

"Let's see. He must be..."

"Thirteen. And never better."

"I hope I'm not interrupting anything. I stopped by for my jacket."

"I planned to drop it off next time I come for coffee. C'mon in. I'm just sorting some pictures I found while unpacking."

She followed him into the living room. He turned on the lamp beside the leather sofa. A woven blanket from his mother hung over the back. Several of his photographs adorned the walls. The evening air wafted through the open screen door.

Cardboard boxes bursting with photographs sat on the floor. There were piles scattered on the coffee table. "I'm trying to organize," he said pointing, "landscape, animals, and people." He pulled a box across the tile floor and sat beside her on the sofa. "There are some pretty old ones in here." He picked up a handful. "Here's one for you." It was a picture of a girl in her preteens standing in front a corral beside an old barn.

"Is that your sister?" She had the longest hair Mim had ever seen, almost to her waist. Mim knew she was a couple years older than Joseph.

He nodded, "Haloke."

Another photo. A boy about eight atop a painted pony. "Is that you? It's hard to tell under that big hat."

"Yup, out riding with my dad." He turned quiet and set the pictures in the "people" pile. Next to it were several photographs of the sky.

She picked up another stack and thumbed through them. Random pictures of desert landscape. Another stack in the middle of the table caught her attention. Stunning pictures. The sun rising over a sheer cliff, trees sticking out of its side. Rocks in a riverbed. The canyon. *Your sanctuary,* Mim thought. She smiled at Joseph, absorbed with the treasure in the cardboard box.

The old pictures stirred memories of their canyon getaway. A photograph of the brilliant half moon. Their campfire. The rocks, a mosaic on the canyon floor. *Oh, what is this?* It was Mim, lying on a blanket near a babbling stream. He got me when I was sleeping? And this? Her heart pounded. He'd caught her laughing, wild hair falling over bare shoulders against the backdrop of the clear afternoon sky. *And, that can't be me.* She was in awe of the reverent beauty. *How did he do that?* Her body melded with the splendor of the canyon.

Joseph watched as she picked up the rest of the pile. More pictures of Mim, stepping out of her jeans, slipping off her shirt, an intimate shot of her naked back.

She eyed the next photo. “Who’s this?” Mim asked. Her eyes grew wide as she recognized this woman with the flowing blond hair laughing up at the camera, provocative with her enlarged breasts and swollen belly. “Oh,” her voice caught in her throat.

“Mim,” Joseph reached for her.

She jerked away, “Addy.” She shook her head, “How did I not know?”

“I wanted to tell you. It was never the right time.”

“No wonder she always puts on that air of ‘I know something you don’t.’” Her jaw clenched. She threw the photographs on the coffee table and strode to the door.

“Let me get your jacket,” Joseph said.

“Good night.” She retreated past Bandit into the night.

Mim turned into her driveway. Numb, she unlocked the heavy front door and shuffled to her room, flopping in a heap on her bed. She was asleep before she heard the familiar tone from her cell phone, a message from Rod.

13

THE ALARM STARTLED MIM from her sleep. She one-eyed her clock; it must have been beeping for twenty minutes. Skipping her morning shower, she brushed her teeth, threw her Cactus Coffee shirt on over a pair of khakis, and tied her hair with a colorful scarf. She saw the message on her cell phone as she scrambled out the door.

"Hey, sleepy head! I was just about to call you." Silkie stood in the hallway by her exercise studio. "I put on a pot," she nodded to the cup in her hand. "You must've had some evening," she observed, "I can't remember the last time you were late."

"Not an evening I want to remember," Mim answered with a look that said, "so don't ask." Silkie held up her hands. Mim entered the coffee shop, so caught up in her thoughts that she didn't thank her friend for turning on the lights and starting the coffee.

At seven o'clock, Mim flipped the sign on the front window to "OPEN." Several minutes later, the Morning Men shuffled in. They filed to the back wall to select their mugs, held them out for Mim to fill at the counter with an uncomfortable, "Good morning" or "How are you, Mim?" and proceeded to their table by the window. She wanted to grab the coffee pot and join them at the table for a little chat. *What have you heard? What business is it of yours?*

Mim was not looking forward to seeing Addy this morning, when she realized that the exercise ladies had not passed through. Were they avoiding her too?

There was an older couple in the shop that she did not recognize. When she brought their breakfast to the table they told her they were camping at Soaring Eagle for a few days.

As soon as everyone had been served, Mim checked what were now two messages from Rod: "Thinking of you. Join me for dinner on Saturday?" Encouraged by his invitation, she glanced at the second sent earlier this morning, "I assume no response means you don't want to join me. I understand."

"There you go again making decisions for me," Mim grumbled. She was about to respond to the text when Silkie called from the hallway, the exercise ladies crowded behind her. Alarmed by her urgent tone, Mim hurried over. "What is it?"

"Ali's missing. Don called Tom. Judith is on her way to the Stevens'. We're going to help search."

Ali? Missing? *Please Lord, let her be safe,* she prayed.

"How about one last warm-up, Mim?" Benny called from the men's table. She grabbed the pot.

"Sorry for eavesdropping," Ralph said, "but did I hear Silkie say something about Ali?" She filled them in. They agreed they had better get out there and help and headed for their cars parked on the street.

Mim stopped by the travelers' table. The woman said, "My, those gentlemen left in a hurry."

"Our friends' daughter is missing," she said, warming their coffee.

"Oh dear!" The woman looked at her husband, "Fritz, I bet that's why those police cars were swarming the park this morning."

Before Mim could respond, Rod's ring tone sounded from behind the counter. "Excuse me, that may be news now," she lied. Thinking of the conflicting texts from Rod, she hesitated, "Hello."

"What's going on? Nini said Ali Stevens is missing."

She began to respond and noticed the couple looking her way. She shook her head and mouthed, "No." They frowned and waved as they left.

As the chimes clanked, Mim said, "Don called Tom at the high school this morning. The whole town is out looking for her."

"Nini said something about a nude selfie Ali sent to her boyfriend. Guess it went viral."

"Is Nini okay?" Mim said. She had not spoken to Nini or Rod since Nini moved out a week ago.

"She's not sure what to think. It's pretty scary."

"I'm sorry I didn't respond to your text last night. I fell asleep," Mim said.

"That's okay. I was hoping you would join me for dinner Saturday."

"Yes, I'd like that."

"Peaceful Pines?"

Their favorite restaurant. "Great. I'll let you know if I hear anything."

The shop was empty and cleaned before two o'clock. Mim was about to flip the sign on the front window to "CLOSED" when Judith sauntered up the walk. "Got a cup o' joe for an exhausted old woman?"

"Your timing is perfect. It's been slow today so I'm closing early. It looks like you get the shop all to yourself. Any news about Ali?"

"No one told you? They found her at the park," Judith slumped into a chair by the window. "Join me and I'll fill you in."

Mim put on a half pot of coffee, then texted Rod to let him know Ali was okay. There was a message from Joseph. Her stomach tensed. "Ali okay. Talk soon." She grabbed the coffee and a couple of mugs from the shelf, anxious to hear the whole story.

Judith, her shoulder-length gray hair pulled back in a festive scarf, looked more relaxed as she gazed out the freshly cleaned window at the town square across the street.

"Another lovely fall afternoon in New Mexico," Mim announced as she approached the table.

Judith sighed, taking the coffee mugs from Mim. "What a day." She rubbed a wrinkled hand across her brow. They sat in the quiet of the shop and sipped the steaming coffee. "That Ali," Judith said, "I don't know what I'd do with her if she were my daughter. Putting her parents through all of that. Poor Karyl was beside herself when she went to wake Ali and found her gone. Car too. Don called the school. And don't you know the kids weren't surprised because by then," Judith stopped.

"They had seen the nude selfie," Mim said.

"You heard, too."

"Nini saw it. She told Rod."

"She saw it?" Judith's face scrunched in disgust. "I don't get kids these days."

"So who found her?"

"Joseph saw her car at the park and notified the police," Judith said. "He and Addy went up the trail and found her in the restroom. Can you imagine, hiding in a filthy restroom?"

Yes, I can, thought Mim. "What a blessing they found her," she said.

"Ali may not agree, having to face her parents."

"I'm sure they were relieved," Mim said.

"I was there when the police called. I could hear Don on the phone with them. To see the joy on his face when he told Karyl their daughter was safe and that she was on her way home."

"And Karyl?"

"I was about to leave when I heard them arguing. Just between you and me, she sounded angry. 'How can we face everyone?' she said."

Sounds like Karyl. “I’m sure it will cause an uproar,” Mim said.

“And she was worried about school. Before I left she asked me if this would effect Ali’s place on the Vietnam Project. I hadn’t thought about it. Could be though, Ali may be so devastated, she may just want to hide.” Judith glanced out the window; a smile crossed her face. “Or maybe not,” she gestured toward the square.

“C’mon, Ali, it’ll be fun! That is what you told me when Mrs. Wilmott brought us here.” Chloe angled her red VW beetle into a parking space by the Splash Pad.

Ali gave her a disgruntled look. “Fun? I don’t know why I let you drag me here.”

“Admit it, you were glad to see me when I showed up at your door. I could see it on your face. You can’t deny it.”

“That is partially true. I would have been glad to see Godzilla just to get away from my mother,” Ali folded her arms across her chest.

“So you were glad to see me,” Chloe said, tilting her head.

“Glad to see you? No, I knew you would have the audacity to show up in person to laugh in my face. I decided I might as well get it over with.”

“I was surprised you let me in,” Chloe said. “To be honest, when I got to school and heard what you did, and saw your selfie...”

"Stop," Ali turned toward the window.

"No listen. Your selfie, your nude selfie, as they are calling it, is not exactly nude. Your arm is totally covering your boobs." She paused, "I was a little disappointed."

"Disappointed?" Ali turned to her, eyes wide.

"Yeah, I thought YOU would have the guts to do a full shot," Chloe pounded her fists on the steering wheel.

"I can't believe this. And I had the tiniest bit of hope that I could trust you. Get me out of here. Take me home."

Chloe assessed Ali to see if she was so fragile that she should take her home. Deciding it best to get things over with, she said, "C'mon Ali. It's the Splash Pad. Washes all your cares away." She mimicked Ali's own words.

Ali looked at her friend, "I appreciate your gesture, but I'd like to go home."

"Okay," Chloe conceded. She spied an elderly white-haired man meandering among the cactus fountains and licked her black-lined lips, "Or maybe you should rescue your demented grandfather."

Surprised, Ali turned to the Splash Pad. Seeing Grandpa Fred looking lost, she bolted from the car. "Grandpa! Grandpa!"

Hearing her voice, Fred Stevens turned, "Alice? Alice, there you are. I've been looking for you." He opened his arms. For a moment, Ali became Alice, a delicate treasure in her great-grandfather's embrace.

From the corner of her eye, she caught Chloe heading for the sprinkler spigot. "Chloe," she boomed.

Her grandfather squealed and grabbed Ali's hands, leaping up and down in the spray. Chloe joined the circle and the trio whooped and cavorted beneath the sparkling sprinkles in a delightful dance.

Ruben, Grace, and Nini were surprised to find Hortensia in the kitchen preparing a pitcher of lemonade when they arrived home from school. She hugged them and ushered them to the patio.

"How was your day?" she asked, trying to appear calm, but their scrutinizing faces cracked her facade.

"What did you hear, Mama?" asked Ruben.

"Tell me about Ali," she was about to burst. "What happened? Did they find her?"

"Yes, Mr. Begay found her," Grace said, "in a stinky bathroom at Soaring Eagle." She held her fingers under her nose. "She caused so much drama. I can't wait to see what the kids do to her when she comes back."

Ruben raised his hand to hush his sister. "Don't be like that. What do you know about her?" He glanced at Nini. She averted her eyes. "Ali sent a picture to her boyfriend last night. On a dare. He sent it to his friend who posted it for everyone to see. She was humiliated and ran away. Kids were laughing about it all day."

Hortensia was confused. "A picture? Why did she run away?"

"It was a nude selfie, Mama," Grace blurted and laughed.

"Selfie?"

"A selfie," Grace said, "a picture of herself on her cell phone. Everyone saw it. What did she expect?"

"Someone from the swim team dared her to send it to her boyfriend, Leonard," Ruben said. "He was shocked and told Gilberto. He didn't believe him so Leonard sent it to him. He never expected Gilberto would send it to everyone."

"Gilberto Peralta? He's a nice boy," Hortensia said.

"It's not a big deal, Mama, kids do it all the time," Grace said.

Ruben's phone dinged. "It's Gustavo, time for practice." He grabbed his gym bag, kissed his mom on the head, and escaped out the back gate.

Hortensia looked from Grace to Nini, "Promise me you will never do something like this. Think of how it looks, think of your parents."

"Mama, we wouldn't do that," Grace said.

"Maybe parents should think of their kids," Nini stood and followed Ruben out the back gate. She marched through the neighborhood massaging the healing scars on the inside of her arm, tears clouding her eyes.

Her steps took her toward the park. She heard the squeals of children on the playground. She was drawn to the swing set where she and Grace often met. Two mothers sat on a bench nearby watching their children.

Mom. I haven't seen you. I haven't returned your texts. Do you miss me as much as I miss you? Nini wondered.

A white SUV passed along the far side of the park. *Mom?* "Mom," she called. Her hope receded with the car down the street.

Mim held the pencil drawing at arm's length, pleased with her work. After a brisk walk at Soaring Eagle, she had spent the past two hours immersed in her art, hoping for a temporary distraction after this trying day, but she was filled with grief without Nini. Risking another rejection, she picked up her phone to text her daughter when she was startled by a loud knock. She opened the large wooden front door and was taken off guard to see Joseph. She was comforted by the sight of Bandit smiling at her from the back of the pickup.

"Evening, Mim," he hugged her as he came through the door, dangling her turquoise jacket.

"Thanks. You didn't need to bring it by."

"You're welcome and maybe I just needed an excuse," he noticed the art supplies on the coffee table. "Am I interrupting? Looks like you're busy, Miss O'Keeffe."

"Not at all," Mim said, guiding him to the sofa in the brightly lit living room. "What a day," she said, plopping down on the leather chair across from him.

He nodded, "You first." He placed his elbows on his faded jeans, his long hair falling like a curtain around his serious face, his black eyes encouraging.

"I tossed and turned all night," she looked at him accusingly, "but this morning I had a text from Rod inviting me to dinner on Saturday. Then Ali disappeared." She closed her eyes and rubbed her hand across her brow, "I don't know what I'd do if Nini ever ran away." They heard Bandit bark as if in agreement.

Joseph stared off. "I'll never forget the look on Ali's face when Addy and I found her." The sound of Bandit whining was like background music. "It broke my heart to see her sitting there on that cold bathroom floor," he closed his eyes. "She looked like a broken baby bird." There was a loud mournful howl, like the soundtrack in a movie. "That dog," Joseph said. He stood. The howling continued. Mim opened the door.

"Bandit. Bandit," Joseph yelled.

Busted. Bandit poked his head around the truck's cab, his feathery tail wagging a truce.

They settled back in the living room. "Where were we?" Joseph said.

"In the bathroom."

"Yes, Addy put her arm around Ali and let her cry. She's amazing with these kids. She has a way about her. When Ali calmed down, Addy reassured her that she was not a bad person. She told her some women love having nude photos taken of them." There was an impish look on his face.

"She did not," Mim stood. "Joseph, this is serious." He moved over and tapped the sofa. She sat beside him.

"Addy persuaded her to going home and promised to stay while she talked to her parents."

"Judith stopped by the coffee shop this afternoon. She said when the police called the look on Don's face was beyond words. But Karyl was more concerned about their reputation." Mim smiled, "You know Judith, she sat her down and told her to stop being so selfish and think of her daughter."

"That's our Judith," he said. His eyes were drawn to the sketch on the table. The sun warming the Splash Pad, the spray of the cactus fountains, two sprites holding hands with an elderly man.

He picked it up. Fred Stevens, with his great-granddaughter, and a grinning girl in black. "This is talent," he said. "You've brought their joyous dance to life." He kissed the top of her head.

"Nothing like what Addy did," she mumbled.

He touched his index finger to her chin and lifted her head. Her muscles tightened. "Let me tell you a story," Joseph said.

He sat back against the sofa, resting his boots on the coffee table. "Thirteen years ago, I was a man in turmoil, throwing myself into my work. Then you arrived with Nini," he shook his head. "Oh, that little girl, such delightful innocence. She opened my heart to laughter and you opened my eyes to the beauty I had created: a sacred space, a haven for others. You gave me hope." He smiled at Mim. She relaxed against the pillow in the corner of the sofa.

"You know I had a rough childhood, struggling to earn my father's approval, failing to be the big little brother my sister needed. Alcohol was available so I drank as a way to escape. I was sent away to boarding school, then Job Corps. I was twenty-six when my sister, Haloke, convinced me to go to rehab. That's where I met Addy." He smiled at the vision of the young, curvy beauty with the sensuous smile.

Addy's an alcoholic? Mim sat up.

He looked her in the eyes, "You know she got pregnant."

Her heart stopped. *Do I want to know this story?*

"When her parents found out they came to the rehab facility. Bob tried to be rational, but Addy's mom, Nancy, was enraged that her daughter had been 'knocked up by a savage,' as she put it." Joseph stared straight ahead. "In the end, it was Bob who saved us."

Bob? Of course, Dr. Freeman.

Joseph clenched his jaw and wrung his hands together. "Nancy had already decided that Addy would have an abortion. But," Joseph sighed, "Bob was heartsick that he had let his little girl down. He thought we should wait until we could make a decision that would be best for the baby, for Addy, and for me." Joseph paused, remembering the horrible scene between Nancy and Bob. Even in Joseph's troubled past, he had never witnessed the vehemence he saw in Nancy that day.

"Several days later, Bob came to visit me." Joseph reached over and touched Mim's arm. "He is such a gentle spirit. He asked me what I wanted to do." He looked her in the eyes. "I didn't know what I wanted, Mim. I couldn't say that I loved Addy, I was so out of it," he shook his head. "After talking with Bob, I did know I wanted our baby to live."

Joseph sat in quiet reflection. "Bob asked about my family on the reservation. I told him that my father, Dark

Wolf, and Silver Feather, my mother, lived there. Also my sister, Haloke, and her husband, James Yazzie. The next day, Bob drove Addy and me to the reservation to meet with my mother," he chuckled.

"Fortunately my father was away. My mother is a very proud woman. I will never forget the anguish on her face when she saw me with Addy. I had disappointed my mother over the years, but this time she was ready to give up. She looked at Bob like he was a crazy man and refused to take the baby. She told me I had brought this all on myself and that the child was my responsibility."

"That must have been difficult for all of you," Mim said.

Joseph nodded, "I felt defeated. I couldn't return to the reservation, not with my father there. But I knew I couldn't give up our baby. Just as we were about to leave, my sister, Haloke, burst through the door. She had seen the fancy car and was worried about my mother. When she saw me she was elated, until she spied Addy. I explained about the baby, that our mother had given her word that this baby would not be raised by her on the reservation. Haloke agreed with our mother. She said, 'this baby will be raised by James and me.'" Joseph leaned toward Mim, "Haloke could not have children. She looked at me with an understanding that this would make up for the loss."

"You gave your baby to your sister?" Mim was trying to make sense of this wild story.

Joseph took her hand, "It was much more than giving our baby to Haloke and James. You don't know Addy's mom. We were afraid she would coerce Addy into have the abortion. So we made a plan. Bob kidnapped Addy." Mim raised her eyebrows in alarm. "He took her to the reservation to live with Haloke and James until the baby was born. When Frank was six months old, Addy returned to the university." He sat up, proud of Addy.

"While she lived on the reservation, Addy volunteered at the clinic and encouraged women to advocate for their families. After she earned her nursing degree, she worked as a pediatric nurse in Albuquerque for ten years. Then her heart took her back to the reservation. She was there until Bob became disabled last spring."

Mim was trying to sort this out. "A son. You and Addy have a son."

"Frank," Joseph's eyes glistened, "Frank Yazzie, twenty-seven years old. Earned his law degree at the university and works with the BIA as a Family Advocate. He has a gift."

After a moment, he picked up the drawing from the coffee table. "You have a gift. You draw life. I can almost hear the music this trio is dancing to." He leaned forward to hug her and Mim looked up at the clock on the wall. "Oh my gosh, it's almost midnight."

"I could stay if you like," he winked.

"I have enough to talk to the therapist about tomorrow." She kissed his cheek and sent him out into the starry New Mexico night.

Her step was lighter as she walked the dark hallway to her bedroom. Turning on the light, she noticed a text on her phone. Rod? she hoped.

Judith. "I want to gather the women. Talk in the AM."

14

THURSDAY MORNING MIM WAS thinking about her appointment with Dr. Sherman. She tried not to let the town gossip get to her. "Don't worry about business," Silkie had said. "It will pick up again once the novelty has worn off."

As Mim took the fresh pot of coffee to the Morning Men's table, she heard Fred's raspy voice, "Good Morning, Mim. Want to see a picture of my granddaughter?"

"She doesn't want to see Ali's picture," Benny said.

Thinking of Ali's selfie, Mim sputtered, and Ralph clarified, "It's her senior picture, Benny."

She stopped by the table of the couple camping at the state park, grateful they were insulated from town gossip.

"We heard they found your friends' daughter at the park yesterday," Velma said. "The excitement will have everyone talking for days."

At mid-morning, Judith breezed through the front door, a big smile on her face. "Good morning, Mim. I saw you got my message last night. I have an idea I want to share with you, if you have a minute." Mim motioned to the empty tables and shrugged. Judith laid a reassuring hand on her arm and said, “Let me see if Silkie can join us.”

As if on cue, Silkie came through the back door, her brown hair in a bun, a striped tunic over her exercise togs. “Did I hear my name?” she raised her eyebrows and hugged both women.

“Judith has an idea for a gathering,” Mim brought coffee and joined them at the square table by the counter.

“Last night I was thinking about the challenges we’ve faced over the past week,” Judith looked at Mim, “and I’d like to have a gathering of women to celebrate in support of one another.”

“What a great idea,” Silkie said, ”celebrate our sisterhood. Do you have a date in mind?”

“Yes, I don’t want to wait. What do you think of next Tuesday?”

“I’m in,” Mim said. “We can meet here tonight to plan if you’d like. The three of us?”

Before Judith could answer, Silkie said, “And Addy?” She looked at Mim.

“Perfect steering committee,” Judith said. “How about seven o’clock?”

“I have an appointment at three,” Mim said, “so seven is fine.” The front door chimes rang. Mim rose. “See you here tonight.”

Mim reflected on her visit with Dr. Sherman as she drove home under a cloak of soft gray clouds. "Call me Maureen," she had said. Mim's stomach had been full of butterflies all day, worried about the session. When Maureen had asked, "What brings you here today?" Mim was surprised by what tumbled out.

"My life is a mess. I threw my daughter out last week. Rod, my ex, told me I should tell her the truth about Rosie and when she found out she called me a liar. I'm empty inside. I've lost everything I ever loved, Rosie, Rod, and now Nini."

Maureen scribbled in the notebook on her lap. "You said, 'the truth about Rosie.' What do you mean?"

Mim thought a moment, then looked at Maureen. "The truth is it's my fault that Rosie died. We were on a walk. I got out my sketchbook and pencils. I got so caught up in my drawing, I wasn't watching. By the time I saw her at the edge of the picnic area, it was too late. The rattlesnake bit her and she died. We told everyone it was an accident."

"What do you mean by that?"

"We told everyone that Rosie and I were hiking and she ran ahead chasing a lizard. We didn't see the rattler at the edge of the trail."

"Why didn't you tell the truth?"

Mim had buried that day long ago. "I was ashamed," she said, "it was easier to lie than to tell the truth. I needed a moment of escape, a moment with my art. I was so focused on myself that I lost my focus on my daughter and she died. I couldn't face that. What would people say?"

"And now Nini knows the truth," Maureen said. Mim nodded. "And how do you feel?"

"It's hard to admit," Mim said, "but I feel free. I don't have to lie anymore."

"What do you want to happen now?" Maureen said.

"I kicked Nini out. I miss her every day. I want her home. And Rod. I want my family back."

Maureen had summarized their first meeting and scheduled another appointment for the following week. She left her with an assignment.

Mim focused on the highway ahead and straightened her shoulders. *I'm going to see Nini tomorrow. And Rod's going to see a side of me he hasn't seen in a long time.* She eyed the colorful bag on the seat beside her. Bella's Boutique. She sucked in her stomach and stuck out her breasts, thinking of the little black dress inside.

The women pulled up to Cactus Coffee just before seven o'clock as if they had synchronized their watches. Judith and Silkie were dressed comfortably in capris and tops. Mim was glad she had not changed out of the dress she had worn that afternoon when she saw Addy alight from Silkie's jeep looking like she was stepping out of a fashion magazine in a short denim skirt, a tight striped tank, heeled espadrilles, and a bright blue scarf adorning her long blond hair. *Why did I think this would be okay?* she wondered.

Mim unlocked the front door and turned on the lights. She brewed the pot of decaf she had prepared that afternoon. The ladies settled around the table against the back wall.

Judith took out a notepad and began, "Last evening I sank into my rocker on the front porch and reflected on the day." The ladies sipped their coffee and enjoyed the pumpkin bars Silkie had brought. "What a commotion created by Ali, disappearing like that, posting that, that," Judith sputtered, "that picture." Silkie looked at Mim and Addy. They grinned.

"Karyl was beside herself with worry. But," Judith tilted her head and pursed her lips, "I think she was more concerned about what people were going to say about her." Judith placed the emphasis on "her." "Bless you and Joseph for finding Ali." Judith patted Addy's hand. "And with all the gossip about you, Mim."

Silkie jumped in, "We're lucky to have each other."

"Yes," Judith said, "and that's when I decided we should have a gathering."

"A meeting, you mean?" Addy said.

"No, not a meeting, a gathering," Judith said, "an informal celebration of women. We can meet right here." She glanced around the shop. Mim nodded. "I looked at my calendar and next Tuesday would be the perfect date."

"Tuesday?" Addy said, "That's in five days. That's hardly enough time."

"It'll work if we start with a small group. And our theme could be 'Mothers and Daughters.' There's nothing like the connection between mothers and daughters."

Mim looked into her coffee mug. *I haven't seen Mom since Easter. I wish she could be here.*

Addy eyed Silkie, *Are you kidding me?* "Mothers and daughters? Sorry, Judith, that might be fine for some, but I think my mother would agree with me on this, we have nothing to celebrate. What do you think, Silkie?"

She didn't want to quell Judith's excitement but she was relieved Addy said something. "It's no secret that the only time I celebrated my mom was three years ago when she died." There was an uneasy silence. "I agree with you, Judith. A gathering is a great idea. Like you said, 'celebrating women.' Let's gather and celebrate our sisterhood."

Judith pointed a finger at Silkie. "Exactly," she said, "our theme can be our sisterhood. We can share stories about the women in our lives."

Addy clapped, "I love it."

"Let's think about who we want to invite and meet tomorrow with our lists," Judith said. "We can contact them over the weekend."

"One of us has a hot date this weekend," Silkie said, pleased with the blush on Mim's cheeks.

"Ooh, a hot date," Judith and Addy said.

"Rod invited me to dinner," she eyed Silkie.

Addy patted Mim's arm. "You have a wonderful, romantic dinner." Mim tensed. Addy leaned closer. "Maybe you can try out the toys you bought at Rhonda's."

"Oh gosh, it's almost nine," Mim said. "We'd better get going if we're going to have our lists ready for morning."

"Thank you, Ladies," Judith said, as the women walked together to their cars. "Good night."

Silkie and Addy chatted about the upcoming event on the drive home and who might come. "Think I should invite my mom?" Addy said.

"If you invite yours, I'll invite mine," Silkie replied. Their relationship with their mothers was a bond they shared. Both of them grew up being tortured by their mothers, never able to live up to their expectations. "We'll be there for each other," Silkie grasped Addy's hand. "It's our sisterhood."

She pulled into Addy's driveway as the neighbor's garage door opened. "I wonder where Rhonda's going at this time of night?"

"Who knows? Perfect timing, though. We can tell her about the gathering." Addy hopped out of the jeep. "Hey Rhonda."

"Maybe not perfect timing," Silkie mumbled.

"Addy, Silkie," Rhonda said. She nodded at the figure in the passenger seat. "You know Wes."

Silkie stammered, "Oh, hi. We um, just wanted to tell you..."

"Tomorrow, we'll talk to you tomorrow." Addy grabbed Silkie's elbow. "In the house," she said, "get in the house."

15

MIM PARKED IN FRONT of the Vega's adobe home. She had texted Hortensia that she would be stopping by. Her stomach tightened as she approached. *Am I welcome here anymore? Will Nini be glad to see me?* she wondered.

The front door opened before Mim rang the bell. "Mim, nice of you to stop by," Hortensia greeted her.

"I was hoping to see Nini," she said, "maybe go for a walk." Squeals sounded from the living room where Grace and Nini competed in a video game.

Hortensia ushered Mim in. "Nini, your mom is here,"

She jumped up. "Mom, what are you doing here?" then pretended she was excited because of the game.

"I'm going out to the park. Would you like join me?"

"It's too hot to go to the park," Nini focused on the TV screen.

"How about a walk around the neighborhood then?" Hortensia said, looking at her daughter for support.

"I can pause the game," Grace said, "go ahead." Nini got to her feet and followed her mother out the door.

The afternoon sun blazed in a sky pebbled with white clouds. Mim put on her sunglasses. “You’re right, it is hot,” she said. “Let’s just go to the school and back.” They walked in silence to the end of the block. “How’s your week been?” Mim said.

Nini kicked a stone up the sidewalk. “Fine.”

“Ali caused a bit of drama running away on Wednesday.”

“I guess.”

“And posting that selfie,” Mim was hoping for a reaction from her daughter.

“I saw it,” Nini wiped the sweat from her forehead with her sleeve.

“Your dad told me. It’s awfully hot for long sleeves.” Nini winced and kicked the stone again. “Let me see your arm,” Mim said.

Nini pulled back the sleeve and stared at her feet. The memory of Wednesday night played in her head. “I just want my mother, I just want my mother,” she repeated the mantra with each step toward home. She had halted in her tracks at the sight of Joseph’s truck in the driveway. Bandit’s loud barking startled her. She approached the truck and nestled her face in the soft shaggy fur of his thick neck, consoled by his whining. “Oh Bandit,” she cooed, “I’ve missed you, Boy.” He barked in response.

“Bandit,” Joseph’s voice had thundered. Nini tore herself away, her heart echoing Bandit’s sorrowful howls floating behind her down the street.

"Oh, Nini, talk to me," Mim reached out to her daughter.

She jerked away. "I saw his truck. You don't care about me," she snarled. "All you care about is Joseph. Just leave me alone." Mim stood in stunned silence and watched her daughter retreat to the shelter of the Vegas home.

16

MIM PARKED BESIDE ROD'S red truck and checked her makeup in the rearview mirror. She ached at the thought of Nini cutting again. Wanting this evening with Rod to be special, she tucked that secret away in her heart.

She noted her reflection in the glass of the front door. Her sassy black dress skimmed her full figure, complimented by the fall colors of the woven pashmina draped over her arm.

Rod greeted her at the door, eying her new dress, "I've made reservations for six," he nibbled her lips, "but we have time for an appetizer here." His hand grazed her thigh.

"Then I will never make it to dinner," Mim reached for the keys in his other hand. "Let's come back for dessert," she said.

"We still think alike," he kissed her again. "I set out some wine in case you want to join me later," he motioned to the bottle and glasses sitting on the coffee table. Mim took his arm, pleased with herself for the overnight bag sitting in the car.

The mood was playful on the drive to Peaceful Pines. They reminisced about other dinners and weekends. "Remember the first time we came here?" Mim said.

"To meet my parents. You played footsie with me under the table. I wanted to grab you and escape to the woods."

"They dragged out the dinner and we were trying to be so polite, but when your mom ordered dessert..."

"I rubbed my belly and said I couldn't eat another bite."

Mim laughed. "Your dad told her it was time to get home and winked at us. I was so embarrassed."

"You didn't act embarrassed when we got home."

Rod pulled into the crowded parking lot. He could not resist the urge to kiss Mim. His lips met hers and he slid his hand under her dress, moaning at the unexpected softness of her flesh. She grabbed his arm, "Mr. Rodriguez, we have dinner reservations."

Rod was still flustered when they sat down to dinner. He ordered their favorite red wine. As they read the menu, Rod felt a tap on his shoulder and was surprised to see Ozzie and Edna Carter, close friends of his parents. "Enjoying a little getaway, you two?" Ozzie said.

"Ozzie, Edna," Rod and Mim greeted them.

"I'm surprised to see you," Edna leaned toward Mim, the smell of alcohol on her breath. "I heard that you threw Nini out."

Mim's mouth dropped open. Rod squeezed her leg under the table. Ozzie closed his eyes and shook his head. He nodded in apology and escorted his wife out of the restaurant.

The waiter brought the wine and filled their glasses. Rod inhaled the bouquet of the claret liquid, eying Mim. "To you, my love," he raised his glass.

"To us," Mim clinked his glass.

Rod studied her. "I want to apologize," he said. "When I supported Nini asking for some time away, I had no idea how disjointed I would feel. I've had time to reflect and I have decided it is you."

"I make you feel disjointed?"

"No," he shook his head, "you are the one who holds us together. When we first met, you pulled all-nighters with me so I could keep up with my studies and play ball. When Rosie died, I didn't want to live anymore," he stared into his lap. "But it was you," he took her hand, "you gave me the strength to keep going. I have always been able to count on you. Since Nini moved out, I feel like I'm falling apart. And then there is you. Somehow I know, I just know, that your inner strength wills us together. I know that Nini will come home, and I..."

"Here we go," the waiter placed the savory entrees on the table and lingered a moment to refill the wine glasses.

"I think that's mine," Mim motioned to the plate in front of Rod. They exchanged dishes, the intimacy of the moment lost.

"I haven't had a chance to tell you," Mim's eyes lit up, "Judith is organizing a gathering."

"About Vietnam? I'd love to go."

"No, it's a celebration of women. Tuesday at the coffee shop."

"Sounds interesting."

"The first gathering is about women supporting women," she paused, "I wish Mom could be there. I've been terrible about keeping in touch with her. I texted her last night out of guilt. I should call her."

"I feel the same way about my dad," Rod said. "The boys have a game tomorrow so I'm taking him with us for a rowdy boys' day."

The waiter came by with the dessert tray. Rod looked at Mim and she blushed. "Everything looks delicious," he said, "but this meal is enough for now." When the waiter turned away they said, "We're having dessert at home."

Rod held Mim's hand during the short ride back to his house. "It's a beautiful night. Have a seat," he motioned to a wooden rocker on the porch, "and I'll bring out the wine."

Rod returned and filled the glasses. "To our future," he lifted his glass.

She touched her glass to his. "To us," she hooked her elbow with his and took a sip, then licked her lips as she gazed at him with twinkling eyes.

17

SUNDAY MORNING ROD PREPARED breakfast burritos and black beans before he had to pick up his dad and the boys. “I’m looking forward to next weekend with Nini,” he said, wiping his mouth with a napkin. “I’m so proud of her. She’s even found a counselor.”

“A counselor? Why didn’t you tell me?”

“I was going to tell you at dinner, but I wanted that to be just about us.” He placed his hand on top of hers. “She called me on Tuesday. There’s someone from the hospital who works with kids at the high school. A Miss Freling, I think, Addy Freling.”

“Addy Freeman?”

“Freeman, you’ve heard of her?”

Mim removed her hand from his. “Yes, I hear she’s an expert in working with teens.”

“Perfect. I haven’t seen Nini since,” he paused, “it’s been almost two weeks. I’m planning a special weekend for us. Have you seen her?”

Caught mid-bite, Mim placed her fork on her plate. “Yes, we went for a short walk Friday.” She had to tell him about the cuts. "She was wearing long sleeves." She looked at Rod.

"I thought her cuts would be healed by now."

"These are new cuts." She blazed on, "I guess Wednesday night, after the drama with Ali, Nini came by the house and saw Joseph's truck."

"He was at the house?" Rod's stomach tightened. "She needed you and you were busy."

"Rod," Mim said.

He threw his napkin on the table, pain searing his heart.

"Let me explain," Mim stared at him.

Rod held up his hand.

Mim slid her chair out, gathered her overnight bag, and marched out the front door.

Rod was steaming as he walked up the steps to his parents' front door and let himself in. "Dad?" he called.

"In the kitchen."

"I know I'm early, but I need to talk to you."

Mando joined his son at the table. "What's going on?"

Rod looked at his father. "I need to apologize, Dad. All these years, you were right about Mim."

"Mim?"

"You told me years ago she was trouble. Remember? I didn't see it. I was so blinded by love. And now, I see you were right. Our marriage went bad, she took Nini away, she was never right for me." He shook his head. "And I was going to ask her to marry me again."

"But," Mando leaned closer.

"But now she's seeing Begay."

"Begay? Didn't he move up north?"

"He's back. And Mim didn't even tell me, Nini did. And the other night Nini went home and his truck was there. I don't know why but I think she's playing me."

Mando sat back in his chair and studied Rod. "I'm the one who was wrong, Son. I always thought you would marry Eva and be a baseball star. Then Mim came along. I saw the way you looked at her. I was afraid I would lose you to the gringa. But Mim always included your mother and me in family plans. Still does. When Rosie died, her world fell apart. She finally looks happy again, when I see her with you."

"I thought so too. Then why was she with Begay?"

"Where were you?" Mando muttered.

A clamor of voices came from the front room. "C'mon Dad," Rod's twins, Ismael and Miguel, burst into the kitchen. "We'll be late for our game."

The overcast sky matched Mim's mood on the forty-five minute drive back to Willow Springs. *How could Rod be so*

loving last night and so distant this morning? Is this what I want? Is it worth the constant turmoil?

She was brimming with negative energy when she got home so she threw in a load of laundry and passed the vacuum over the tile floors. There wasn't much cleaning to do since she was living alone now.

Hungry and ready for a break, Mim was browsing for some ham and cheese in the fridge when she heard the crunch of tires on the gravel driveway. *Maybe Silkie is stopping by to talk about the gathering,* she thought.

She glanced out the window at the silver sedan. Yoli? *What is Rod's mom doing here? Maybe she came to see Nini.* She opened the front door to welcome her. A spry woman with a salt and pepper pixie emerged from the passenger side, her rosy lips curved in a warm smile. "Mom," Mim wrapped her arms around her. "What are you doing here? I'm so happy to see you."

"Oh Sweetheart, Rod called last week with a plane ticket and chauffeur service from the airport," she winked at Yoli. "He thought you might need a little company."

Mim's heart tightened, wondering if he would have done the same thing today. She fixed two more sandwiches, poured iced tea, put some grapes in a bowl, and followed them to the patio. They chatted about Irene's trip and the weather, which had been so pleasant for September.

Irene said, "How are things going with Nini?"

"About the same, I'm afraid. I saw her Friday for a short walk. She still doesn't want to talk."

"What are you going to do? She can't stay there forever," Irene said.

Mim grimaced. Yoli changed the subject. "How was your dinner with Rod last night?" she asked, a gleam in her eye.

"Who doesn't love Peaceful Pines?" Mim said. "Our dinner was delightful." Irene and Yoli leaned closer, but Mim denied them the conflicting details.

"Do you mind if I stop by to see Nini while I'm in town?" Yoli said. "I haven't seen her since she started school."

"I'm sure she'd love it," Mim said.

"Can I tell her you're here, Irene?"

"Sure. Tell her I'll bake her some of my chocolate drop cookies."

The ladies put the dishes in the kitchen and escorted Yoli to her car. Mim hugged her, "Thanks for being Mom's chauffeur."

"My pleasure. It gave us a chance to visit before Mando and I leave on our trip to Mexico."

"I can't believe it's time for your annual visit," Mim said. "Give my love to everyone." She and Irene waved as Yoli backed out of the driveway.

"We'll put you in the guest room, Mom," Mim said, wheeling Irene's suitcase down the hall.

"Thanks," Irene said. "I think I'll get settled in and take a little nap," she yawned. "Let's go to supper later and maybe a walk at the park. Keep these old bones moving." She hugged her daughter.

Mim's anger at Rod mixed with gratitude. He knew just what she needed, a visit with her mother. She wanted to call him, but decided a text might be better, "Mom is here. Thank you so much."

18

MIM WAS PLEASED TO see her mother up early on Monday morning, offering to join her in the coffee shop. When Silkie peeked in and saw Irene, she squealed and burst into the shop, embracing her in a Silkie hug. "Irene, what brings you here? Tell me you're moving back to New Mexico," Silkie and Irene swayed back and forth.

"I heard something about a gathering and I couldn't miss it."

"Perfect. Our guest list is complete. I'm off to class, but I'll catch you when I get back." Silkie sauntered out the back door.

Thanks for your help, Mom, Mim thought. She was preparing coffee drinks for two moms who had dropped off their kids at the elementary school down the street. Irene had offered to warm up the coffee for the Morning Men and now she sat at their table, between Fred and Ralph.

The chimes rang. Rhonda strolled into the shop and proceeded to the counter. She cocked an eyebrow at the woman sitting with the Morning Men, "Good morning, Mim."

"Nice to see you, Rhonda." Mim nodded at the men's table, "My mother, Irene. Showed up yesterday. A surprise from Rod," she smiled. "She told Silkie she heard about our gathering."

Rhonda took her steaming latte from Mim. "That's wonderful. I can't wait. See you tomorrow night."

Mim was putting on another pot of coffee when Silkie and Marie showed up at the counter. "Whew, this woman worked us hard today," Marie wiped sweat from her forehead.

"You need to stay fit to keep up with those grandchildren," Silkie said. "Looks like it's just the two of us today, Mim. I'll have my usual white mocha, please."

"I'll have the same," Marie said and followed her friend to the table by the window. "I heard you ran into Wes the other night." She was amused by the "You know about that?" look on Silkie's face. Marie sighed, "It's a relief to be able to talk about it."

The ladies had their heads together in quiet conversation when Mim delivered their coffee. She moved on to help her mother clearing the table vacated by the Morning Men.

Marie rested her hand on Silkie's arm. "Poor Wes. He felt so guilty. Thank goodness it was you who caught them. You're one of the few people around here who doesn't gossip."

Silkie nodded.

"You know how ruthless you can be about me babysitting my grandchildren?"

"Yes," Silkie squirmed.

"When Wes was diagnosed with prostate cancer, I retired from teaching and devoted every moment to his recovery. After his treatment, I had no purpose and you suggested I do whatever made me happy. I enjoy my grandchildren, but I taught for forty years and I raised two daughters. I don't want to raise my grandchildren."

Ouch, Silkie flinched.

"You know it's hell going through chemo and radiation. And they never tell you the side effects can be even worse."

Silkie touched her hand to her chest, an unconscious gesture following her battle with breast cancer. She recalled the violent bouts of nausea, the mental trauma of the double mastectomy, the slow recovery after radiation and reconstruction.

"It was devastating for Wes, for us, because," she leaned very close and whispered, "it left him unable to perform." She glanced between her legs. "We stopped communicating and found things to do on our own. Wes spent time golfing, I went to visit the girls."

Silkie placed a supportive hand over Marie's.

"That's where Rhonda came in," Marie said. "She and Wes ran into each other at the golf course and began talking. You remember her struggle with breast cancer."

"At twenty-eight years old," Silkie said. "She's something, my role model."

"Mm-hmm," Marie nodded, "and she listened to Wes. She knew what he was going through. They started spending time together and eventually became intimate." Silkie raised her eyebrows in understanding. “I noticed the change in Wes, he had more life in him. When I mentioned it, he confided in me.”

“What did you do?” Silkie said.

“I felt betrayed. I couldn’t understand. I turned away. And then,” she studied the coffee mug in her hand, “I met a man at church.”

“At church?” Silkie wrinkled her nose, “Don’t tell me this was God’s idea.”

Marie shrugged her shoulders. “His wife passed away a year ago from cancer. We connected. And Wes was seeing Rhonda.”

“You’re having sex with this guy?”

“I like the attention, the physical contact.”

“What about Wes?”

“He knows. We have an agreement. We don’t talk about Rhonda or Randy.”

“Randy?” *You’re not serious,* Silkie thought. “Rhonda and Randy? Sounds like a comedy team.” Both women laughed.

“Thank you, Silkie. I needed this,” Marie said. “Things are better now. Wes and I talk, and we listen to each other. We do more together.”

“That’s right,” Silkie said, “you’re taking a trip to Costa Rica after Christmas.”

Mim was picking up dishes at another table. Marie caught her eye, “I’m looking forward to Judith’s gathering here tomorrow night.”

“Should be some event,” Mim said.

19

MIM AND IRENE ARRIVED at Cactus Coffee before the Gathering. The wreath on the door added a festive touch. Mim flipped on the lights. “I like the way you’ve arranged the room, Mom. Pulling those five tables close together creates an intimate space.”

“Thank you.” Irene set the platter of homemade cookies on the counter beside the pot of yellow mums. She lit the candles on each table and turned on the floor lamps she had placed strategically around the room. “Are you ready?” She turned off the overhead lights. A soft glow warmed the room.

“Mom, it’s elegant,” Mim said. “I love the gourd centerpieces and, mmm,” she inhaled, “is that pumpkin?”

“Toasted pumpkin. I hoped you’d like it,” Irene said.

“I do. I wish I had your knack for creating such inviting spaces.”

“The opportunity was always there,” Irene said, ”you preferred spending time in the studio with your father.”

The front door chimes rang as Judith, Addy, and Silkie entered the shop. “Oh, Mim, it’s gorgeous,” Silkie said.

"It wasn't me," Mim nodded at her mother standing in the middle of the tables, a warty orange gourd in her hand.

"Of course. Thank you, Irene."

"Smells like fall," said Addy, looking like autumn in a short rust-colored dress, complemented by an eye-catching yellow, olive, and orange beaded necklace.

Judith stood behind them. "Just lovely," she said. "I brought something for you." She moved to the counter, unveiling Mim's drawing of Ali, Fred, and Chloe in a handsome rustic frame. "There," she said.

A spark ignited in Mim's heart. "Oh Judith, thank you." Silkie patted Mim's back. Irene busied herself with the decorations on a nearby table.

Rhonda burst through the front door, dressed in a long flowing skirt and denim jacket. "Oh my goodness," she said, "Cactus Coffee transformed."

"Rhonda," Addy greeted her.

"Hi everybody," Rhonda said. "I brought my mom." She took the elbow of the woman beside her, a tall, large framed woman, the ends of her dark hair curling up at her shoulders. "I thought she'd enjoy this too."

"Bea," Silkie hugged Rhonda's mom.

"You know Addy," Rhonda said, "and this is Judith, who had the fabulous idea for the gathering, and Mim, the owner of this delightful shop, and..." She nodded at the woman who was straightening a chair.

"That's my mother, Irene. She was here yesterday when you came for your coffee."

"That's right. Irene, you were flirting with the Morning Men."

Irene blushed, "Nice to meet you." She invited Bea to the counter for refreshments as Karyl arrived, followed by Marie and Ellen.

"Welcome ladies," Judith stood in the center of the tables, arms outstretched. "Please help yourself to refreshments, find a seat, and we'll get started."

Karyl joined Judith at the end table. Mim sat at the table next to them with her mother. Addy and Silkie sat at the head of the semicircle, with Ellen and Marie beside them, leaving the last table for Rhonda and Bea.

"Thank you all for coming," Judith began.

Two figures approached the coffee shop. *They must think we're open,* Mim thought. A petite round woman in a crimson blouse and long black skirt, her steel gray hair tied in a bun, strode into the coffee shop. Mim's eyes lifted to the woman behind her. She looks just like...

"Silver Feather, Haloke," Silkie greeted the newcomers and escorted them to Addy's table. Addy hugged them, a proud look on her face.

Silkie set her coffee mug and cookie plate next to Irene. Mim raised her eyebrows. *You invited Joseph's family?* Silkie grinned.

"Welcome to our gathering," Judith began again. "I am Judith Wilmott. I was the Director of the Library here in Willow Springs for forty years before my retirement three years ago." Everyone applauded. "I am constantly in awe of the community we have here," she looked at Karyl and Mim, "and especially grateful for the friendship and support of the women. So," she smiled at Mim, "I asked Mim if we could gather here to celebrate the women in our lives. Or as Silkie says, 'Celebrate our Sisterhood.'" Addy and Marie clapped. "Let's begin with introductions. Then we'll open it up to anyone who would like to share about the special women in their lives. Karyl, will you start us off, please?"

Karyl rose. "I'm Karyl Stevens. My family has called New Mexico home for over a century. My husband, Don, and I have been married for twenty-seven years. We have two children." She stood tall as she looked around the circle of women. "I have always counted on my family. It was only recently that I was reminded how fortunate I am to have the support of many women in our community."

"Thank you, Karyl," Judith said. "Let's just go around the circle this way." She motioned to her right.

Mim stood. "I'm Mim Rodriguez. Welcome to my coffee shop." Silkie clapped. "I grew up in Artesia. I went to NMSU and moved here thirteen years ago with my daughter, Nini." She put her hand on Irene's shoulder. "This is my mother, Irene Johnstone. She surprised me when she arrived from Kansas City on Sunday. The table decorations are her contribution." Mim motioned at the tables.

"And I baked the cookies," Irene said.

"Yes," Mim smiled, "her famous chocolate drop recipe. You must try them."

Silkie was followed by Addy. "I'm Addy Freeman. I grew up here in Willow Springs and moved away when I went to college. I recently returned to care for my father who had a dental practice here for many years." She clasped her hands and looked at her guests. "Most of you know Joseph Begay," she glanced around the group. "This is..."

Haloke rose. "Silver Feather, Addy's mother-in-law; and I am Joseph's sister, Haloke." Silver Feather rested her arm on the back of Addy's chair. Mim was intrigued by her exquisite silver ring.

Marie and Ellen introduced themselves and Rhonda was the last to stand. "I'm Rhonda Kellerman, the mammogram technician at the hospital."

"And our resident sex toy therapist," Addy mumbled.

"I grew up in Willow Springs. A few years behind Addy." She grinned, "and this is my mom, Bea. She came for the evening from Las Cruces and left my father to fend for himself." There was laughter around the room. "I'm so glad she could be here with me tonight."

"Thank you," Judith said. "From the looks on peoples' faces, we've all learned something new this evening. What a blessing to belong to such a sisterhood, to know that we can count on each other, especially when we are at our lowest." Judith looked around the semicircle. Her eyes rested on Ellen.

"I'd like to thank a dear friend tonight. Many of you know I came to be the town librarian after my husband, Lee, was listed as missing in action in Vietnam. I was suffering from terrible depression; I didn't even get out of bed some mornings." The discomfort in the room was evident, but the women kept their eyes on Judith. "One day a friend called and said, 'Come to Willow Springs. We could use your talents here and I would welcome your friendship.' My life began anew that day. Thank you, Ellen."

Rhonda stood. "I'd like to share. I was diagnosed with breast cancer fourteen years ago." Bea took Rhonda's hand. "I didn't think I could go on." She let the tears run down her face and squeezed her mom's hand. "Mom, you listened without judging and pushed me when I wanted to quit. You encouraged me to pursue my dream as a mammography technician. It has become my mission, as a cancer survivor, to walk alongside others when they face debilitating health challenges. Thank you, Mom. Thank all of you," she looked around the circle, "for your never-ending support."

After a moment, Silver Feather stood. At just five feet, she had an air of subtle power. "Thank you for inviting me to your gathering tonight. I am pleased to be here with my two daughters," she looked to her left at Haloke, and her right, at Addy. "I've had many blessings in my seven and a half decades," her rough voice was soft, yet commanding, "you have given me the most precious gift, my grandson, Frankie." She rested her arms on Haloke and Addy's shoulders, tears of pride glistening in her eyes. "Frankie brings such joy. He is an intelligent, strong, and kindhearted man. He is a blessing to me, our family, and our people. Thank you, My Daughters."

Silkie stood and looked around the room. "I am grateful for the women who support me and make me feel like I belong. I appreciate each of you." She walked over to the counter. "I would like to recognize the talent of one among us," she pointed to the drawing of the dancers. "I am proud of you, Mim, for allowing your passion to live again." The ladies all stood. Everyone but Karyl and Irene clapped.

A delightful chatter filled the coffee shop during the fellowship following the event. Bea gushed to Irene, "These cookies are delicious. You could sell them."

Mim took a cookie from the platter. "Right? These are my favorites," she said. She felt a hand on her arm.

Silver Feather stood beside her, studying Mim's drawing. "You are a true artist, Dear. I have a favor to ask you." Mim tensed. "I'd like you to draw a portrait for me, of my Frankie."

"I'd be honored," Mim said. "Do you have a picture I can have?"

"On my cell phone," Silver Feather reached into her pouch.

"I can't help but admire your ring," Mim pointed.

Silver Feather held out her left hand, "It was given to me by my mother-in-law. It is a tradition that when a mother accepts the woman her son chooses to marry, she passes on the ring." She smiled at Mim. "I am still waiting on that son of mine."

Addy stood behind them. "What are you two up to? Secret plans?"

"I was just telling Mim how impressed I am with her drawing."

Addy pointed, "My favorite is the one on the back wall."

Silver Feather surveyed the drawing of the entrance to Soaring Eagle State Park where her son worked and glanced back at the Splash Pad sketch. "You have great talent. You should not be hiding these pieces. You should be sharing them."

"You could sell them," Addy said.

"You should," Silkie joined them.

"Sell her sketches?" Irene broke into their little circle. "But she has such a lovely coffee shop here. This is truly her niche."

"She does more than bake cookies," Addy muttered.

"I love my coffee shop," Mim said. "Drawing is just a hobby."

"You never know. People might really like your stuff." Silkie tilted her head. "What if we give it a try? Have an art show?"

The excitement from the group attracted the attention of the others. "An art show, did you say?" It was Rhonda's voice. "That's a fabulous idea. We could have an impromptu art show. Soon."

"Yes, today is Tuesday. How about Sunday?" said Marie.

"That's too soon. How about the following Sunday?" Rhonda said.

"And we can have it here, like the gathering," Judith chimed in. "We can get word out, post signs around town." The women nodded.

"Ladies, ladies," Mim raised her voice, "I appreciate your enthusiasm, but this is my artwork you're talking about. Who said I would like to show it?"

"Of course you want to show it," Judith said.

Mim looked at the women, staring at her. Her heart thumped in her chest. "I used to show my work."

"And you won several awards, didn't you?" Silkie said.

"That was a long time ago. I'm a different person now. I like my life. I like what I do." Mim's heart pounded. Even as she spoke, she knew she was lying.

"You ladies all mean well, I'm sure," said Irene, "but Mim gave up drawing years ago. I'm sure she doesn't have much that's worth showing."

Mim looked at her mother and thought about the frenzy with which she had been drawing since Nini moved out. The passion imprisoned inside seemed to pour onto the page.

"I disagree," Addy said, "I think a select display of Mim's work could be quite powerful."

"I can't, I just can't." Mim turned away.

"You could at least let us look at some of your work. I bet you have pieces people would love to see," Judith said. The women agreed.

Silver Feather was at Mim's side. "You've denied your gifts for many years now. Perhaps it is time to share them." Mim looked into Silver Feather's eyes. Joseph's eyes. Eyes that saw into her soul. "You can think about it," she said.

"No," Mim said.

"Okay," Judith shook her head. "But I think you're making a mistake. Let people see the hidden you."

"I mean, no, I don't need to think about it," Mim said. "I'll do it. If you will all help me."

There was a cacophony of excited voices.

Judith looked around the group. "I'll be in charge of the planning. Let me get organized and I will let you know what you can do to help." It was settled.

Mim was exhausted and exhilarated when she climbed into bed. Could she do this? Her mother didn't seem to think so, but Silver Feather's words repeated in her head, "Perhaps it is time." *What will Rod and Nini say?* she wondered as she drifted off to sleep.

20

MIM SAT WITH IRENE on the patio, eating the broccoli chicken casserole and fresh bread Irene had prepared. "Judith stopped by today," Mim said, "with plans for the art show." Irene watched a hummingbird flitting at the feeder. "She's going to ask the high school kids for help. She has an idea for a flyer that the art class can make. The students in the Vietnam project will be ambassadors, serving food and greeting people."

"That Judith is a go-getter. First she organized the women's gathering and now your art show. Don't you think it might be a little too much for her? All at once?"

"Not at all. When Judith decides to do something, it's best to keep out of her way." Mim's phone buzzed on the table. "It's Rod. I can call him later."

"No, Honey, go ahead. I'll get the dishes started," Irene said, gathering the plates.

"Hi, Rod. No, Mom and I just finished dinner." As Mim listened, her brows knit together, "Nini told you about my art show?" Irene heard Rod's muffled reply. She picked up her glass with her free hand and escaped through the back door.

"I didn't realize how much I've missed my art. I haven't shown my work in years. It's a dream come true, but I'm so nervous." Mim listened. She frowned. "I hope you can be there. Let me know after you talk with Eva." She clenched her teeth. "Thank you. I love you, too." Mim ended the call and sat a moment. *Eva,* she thought, *please cooperate just this once. I need Rod there with me.*

"Mom?" Mim entered the kitchen, "Rod said you saw Nini."

Irene put the glasses in the top rack of the dishwasher. "I made her some cookies," she said.

"You didn't tell me," Mim stared at her mother. That fall morning the day after Rosie died replayed in her head, like a dark film. Nini was teething so Irene took her for a walk. She returned a short while later with Nini sound asleep. Rod had cradled the baby in his arms and taken her to her room.

Irene followed Mim into the apartment carrying the backpack she had found in the stroller. She reached into the open bag. "I found this," she said, "your drawing of our precious Rosie."

Mim took the mud-smudged picture from her mother. "I, I," she stammered, "I couldn't help myself. I had to get my pencils out. It was a beautiful day and she was having so much fun playing in the water."

"Who?" Rod came down the hallway.

Mim looked from Rod to Irene, blinking back tears. "Rosie. Yesterday. I, I was drawing Rosie," she choked, "and when I looked up..."

"You were drawing?" Rod was perplexed. "Why didn't you tell me?" His thoughts whirled. *I thought I was being punished for making you take her.*

"I'm so sorry," Mim cried. "There wasn't time. I just wanted to save my daughter." She clutched the drawing to her heart.

It was Irene who said, "No one needs to know. They think it was an accident."

"It was an accident," Mim said.

Rod looked through her, "If you hadn't been drawing."

"It was an accident," Irene was insistent. "No one needs to know."

"Honey?" Irene waved the plate she was holding at her daughter.

Mim looked at her mother; her heart was numb. "It was you," she said. "When Rosie died, you told me not to tell anyone I was drawing," her voice was flat, "you told me to lie. Why, Mom?"

The plate in Irene's hand fell to the floor and shattered. She stared down at the debris and shook her head. "I should have kept you in the kitchen."

Irene took a deep breath and looked at Mim. "Your father, the artist," her eyes were dreamy, "Oh, when I met him, he swept me off my feet with that free spirit of his. I was enamored, coming from such a regimented family. Against their warnings, I ran away and married the love of my life, only to find out too late that painting was the love of his." She stared off for a moment. "I doted on your brother because he loved everything that was not art. But you, you wanted to be in the studio with Levi. I tried to interest you in the kitchen. Remember I made us look-alike aprons?"

"With the cookies on them? I loved mine," Mim said.

"And you wore it straight out to the studio," Irene said. She peered out the back door. "I hate art. I lost your father to his painting and I lost you to your drawing."

"Oh, Mom," Mim reached out to her mother. Shards crunched under her foot.

Irene held up her hand, "And because of that, I lost my granddaughter, too. I've felt guilty all these years. My Rosie would still be alive if I'd kept you in the kitchen."

21

IRENE STRETCHED OUT ON the sofa and rubbed her stomach, "I ate too much at Tom and Silkie's. I'm stuffed. I think I'll relax and watch a little TV."

"Silkie makes the best chili, doesn't she?" Mim said. "Mind if I go to my room? I'd like to pick out some drawings to show Judith on Sunday."

Mim pulled the portfolios from the back of the closet and sat on the tile floor beside the bed. The maroon folder was filled with drawings from her early days with Rod, until Rosie died. Then she had punished herself by putting her art tools away.

When she moved to Willow Springs, she had purchased a gray portfolio, after she drew the Soaring Eagle at the state park, with the hope that healing might be possible. She squeezed the cardboard folder. It felt almost empty. She opened it and flipped through the drawings.

This is a good one, Mim thought, pulling out a drawing of Cactus Coffee from the Square, right before it opened. *I love the big planters in the front, the awning above the front window, and my favorite part, the cactus holding the coffee cup on the stained glass door.* She placed it in the "Show" pile.

There were a few drawings of the state park, on a sunny day, after a storm, in the stark winter. *Ooh, this is a good one,* she thought, holding up the sketch of Joseph in his truck with five year old Nini waving out the passenger window and Bandit sitting tall in the bed. She held it a moment before adding it to the "Show" pile.

There was the drawing of Nini she had done last month in front of the hallway mirror checking out her new outfit for the first day of school. Mim had stood behind her thinking, I can't believe she's going to high school. *I hope she likes this one.* She put it in the "Show" pile.

Behind it was the drawing she had expended all of her tears over after Nini left. There was Mim melted into the tile floor, the images of Rod and Rosie and Nini etched into the edges. "You can stay right there," she said. But the small square tucked in front of it, she smiled, the sketch she had made of Bandit's head when Joseph brought her home from the Night Sky Event. "Show."

She picked up the hefty portfolio of her early work. *Am I ready?* she wondered, remembering the afternoon when Nini discovered the last drawing of Rosie, the day Mim's world imploded. She took a deep breath, *perhaps it is time.*

Her heart filled with pride as she scanned the work in the folder, drawings she had made out of love. Nini in her Easter dress, Mim placed in the "Show" pile. Yoli teaching Rosie to make tortillas, dusted head to toe in flour, that mischievous grin on her face, "Show." Rod in his baseball uniform, "Show." The drawing of Nini, Bandit, and Joseph in his truck. She placed it in the "Show" pile, and paused.

Joseph's truck. What did I do with that? She got a chair from the corner and looked up on the top shelf of her closet. *There it is.* The blue "private" portfolio.

She looked over at her door. She heard noise from the TV, her mom must still be watching. She opened the portfolio and looked through the drawings. Rod in class, Rod at the White Sands, Joseph in the canyon. Here it is, Joseph in his truck.

Was it really seven years ago? It seemed like yesterday. Mim felt the ache in her heart. She was returning from a class walk when she spotted his truck parked back off the road. When the class left, she returned and found Joseph slumped over the steering wheel. "Joseph," she called fearing he may be dead. He looked out at her, eyes swollen and red. "Joseph, what happened?" She spotted the bottle of whiskey between his legs.

"My father," he said. "My father is missing. He's been stabbed."

Mim was horrified, but she waited.

"My nephew caught him beating my mother, threatening her with a knife. He grabbed his knife and stabbed him in the side and in the back. My father lashed out, cut my nephew's jaw open, then got in his truck and rode off into the desert."

"Your father stabbed him? Certainly no father..."

Joseph pulled back his sweaty black hair exposing a messy scar where his ear had been.

"Your father?" Mim said, struggling to find words.

"I walked in the barn one day. I was twelve. I heard grunting. Then," Joseph rested his forehead against the steering wheel. After a moment, he looked up. He stared out the windshield, "He was raping her, my sister, Haloke."

Mim placed her hand on his shoulder.

"I grabbed my knife and hollered as I thrust it at him, cutting his arm. He lurched back and sliced at my head."

"I never knew."

"And what good did it do? I wasn't there. I wasn't there for my mother, for my nephew, for my father." He lifted the whiskey bottle from between his legs.

"Joseph," Mim put her hand on the door ledge.

He looked at her, the life gone from his eyes. He unscrewed the cap.

"What good will it do anyone if you do this?" She pointed at the bottle. "Listen to me. Right now you can be there for them. Give me that bottle and go home."

He put the bottle to his lips, then he threw it out the passenger window. Mim could still hear the smash of the glass as it hit the ground.

"Honey, what are you doing up there?"

Mim jumped. "Oh Mom, you startled me. I was just looking for something." She motioned to the piles on the floor. "I've got a good start, don't you think?"

Irene tilted her head at a hodgepodge on the floor. "I think you do. I'm going to bed unless you need some help," Irene offered. Mim shook her head. "Then I'll see you in the morning."

"Good night, Mom."

Mim looked at the drawing of Joseph again. The way she had drawn his forehead against the steering wheel, his long hair covering his face, no one would know it was he. She held the picture against her heart, then slid it into a separate folder with the restored drawing of the Soaring Eagle.

Mim felt renewed after browsing through the years of work she had hidden away. *It is time,* she thought, *time to share who I am. This art show is the perfect start.*

She gathered up the drawings and placed them with the chair back in the corner and returned the portfolios to the closet. She picked up the folder of blank pages, shades of white and soft hues and found a sheet of smoky brown. "Hello Frank," she said. She set it aside thinking, *if I begin the portrait tomorrow, I can finish in time for the art show.*

Before bed that evening, Mim texted Rod, "Gathered drawings for my show. Love you."

"Can't wait to see them. Sweet dreams."

22

BY THE TIME JUDITH came by on Sunday afternoon, Mim had set aside sixty pieces that she thought would make a meaningful display. Judith was impressed. “Mim, I knew you were talented, but I had no idea. Look at these; they are true masterpieces. You have such a gift.”

They made plans for the presentation of the pictures. Some would need matting, some needed frames, some would stay as they were.

“We can hang some on the walls and display some on easels,” Judith said. ”Ellen and I are going to Las Cruces on Tuesday to get materials. Let’s meet at the coffee shop when we get back to mat and frame the pictures. Irene, why don’t you join us?” She looked at the housedress Irene was wearing. “We’ll all need new outfits. This is a big event.”

That evening, Mim pulled up the photo of Frank that Silver Feather had sent her and studied the outline she had started. The dark thoughtful eyes she had drawn stared back at her. The eyes of his father.

I'd love to finish this before the show to surprise her, Mim thought. She picked up a medium point pencil to begin the nose. Her phone dinged, a text from Rod. "I miss you. Meet me for dinner Tuesday?"

She texted back, "Yes. Can't wait to tell you about the show. See you Tuesday. Love" and pressed "Send."

Oh, not Tuesday. She typed again, "Prepping for show Tuesday. Therapy Thursday. Wednesday?" *Please say you can make it Wednesday.*

Her phone dinged. "I have to take the boys to practice Wed. Can you change your schedule?"

Maybe Judith would be able to meet on Wednesday, Mim thought. *But she's already set the plans. When Judith speaks.* "No," she texted, "plans made. Can someone else take the boys to practice?"

"No, Wednesday is my night with the boys. Guess we'll have to wait until Sunday."

"I have to take the boys," Mim said. "I have to take the boys." She looked at the pile of drawings on the chair for the art show and the drawing on the easel. *I'll put all my energy into the show,* she thought, *you'll be so impressed.*

She picked up her pencil and turned her attention back to the portrait of Frank Yazzie. He had Joseph's straight nose, but the upturn was definitely Addy's. Mim shook her head and pressed her pencil to the smoky brown paper.

23

"HOW DO I LOOK?" Irene entered the kitchen wearing the new outfit she bought in Las Cruces.

"I love the top. The greens really set off that fancy new hairdo Judith suggested. And cute capris. I thought you and Judith were going to Ellen's for dinner. Looks more like you're headed for a night on the town."

Irene curtsied. "I think we'll have more fun at Ellen's. Friday is poker night so Chet will be out with the boys."

Mim stood in her bedroom before the portrait on her easel. "Hey, Frank, you're looking good, young man," she said.

Two days until the art show. Everything was ready. Drawings matted and framed waiting in Nini's room to be set up tomorrow afternoon. She would complete her final project, the portrait of Frank, tonight.

She held the image on her phone next to the portrait on the easel, humbled by the opportunity to create this sacred work for Silver Feather. *Joseph's son.* She noted the distinct nose. *And Addy's son,* she thought.

Mim felt alive again, filled with passion for her work. Her heart was softening, beckoning hope.

Mim looked at the thick brown hair that swept over his forehead and fell a few inches below his collarbone. Her pencil glided over the paper as she drew and shaded. There. She stepped back.

"One last thing." She took a deep breath and rested her pencil at the midpoint of his right jaw. With care she drew the sharp line of the scar that dipped at his chin.

Mim put the finishing touches on the picture and said a silent prayer. She signed her name, then blessed the portrait, "For you, Silver Feather. Your Legacy." She stood in silence with her hand over her heart. The screen on her phone lit up. Rod calling. She waited. The light went out.

Her heart torn, she called back. "Hi. I'm sorry I couldn't get to my phone. How are you?"

"Sorry it's late. I just got back from taking the boys to camp. I hope you weren't sleeping."

"No, I was just..." Her eyes went to the portrait on the easel, "putting last minute touches on the show."

"I can't wait to see it," Rod said.

"I'm looking forward to sharing it with you. And Nini. She texted that you bought her a new outfit for the show."

"I did. It's a special occasion."

"You're making me nervous." Mim said.

"Don't worry. We'll be there with you."

24

CACTUS COFFEE WAS ABUZZ on Saturday morning with talk of the art show. Ralph sat with Chet and Ellen and Fred at the Morning Men's table. They invited Irene to join them. Mim snickered when Ralph said, "No Fred, she does not want to see a picture of your granddaughter."

Silkie stopped in after her aerobics class. "Lots of energy in here today. Everyone's gearing up for the big event. How are you doing?"

"I'm a little nervous, but Rod and Nini are picking Mom and me up for the show."

"Tom and I are anxious to see your work," Silkie said. "To hear Judith talk, you'd think you're the next Frida Kahlo."

The campers from Soaring Eagle were there. "We're looking forward to your art show," Velma said. "Will any of your work be for sale?"

"Not at this show, " Mim said. "I don't really know what to expect since this is my first show. Who knows what may happen?"

Mim and Irene were bringing in the last boxes of artwork from the back hallway when Judith arrived. She and Mim set up the display, while Irene arranged the cookies she had made on platters, wrapped them and returned them to the fridge.

"You don't want that there," Irene heard Judith's voice and looked out to see her pick up the drawing Mim had positioned on the welcome table inside the door. "It looks like the entrance to the state park, not your art show." She replaced it with the frame in her hand. "Your portrait goes there. This will look better on the counter, don't you think?"

"Are you ready, Honey?" Irene emerged from the back. She paused, "Judith, this place is amazing. What an eye-catching exhibit."

"Thank you," Judith said, "most of the arrangement was Mim's idea." Irene exchanged a glance with her daughter. "I just need to hang that last picture over the refreshment table."

"Oh Judith, you've done so much already. We can get that. You save your energy," Irene reached behind the counter to retrieve Judith's purse, "you'll need it for the show tomorrow."

"How's this, Mom?" Mim adjusted the frame on the wall.

"It's perfect," Irene said, surveying the room. "Honey, your dad would be so proud of you." She picked up the picture of the soaring eagles from the counter where Judith had placed it. "And I'm sure he'd agree," she handed the picture to Mim, "this belongs on the welcome table."

25

MIM WOKE EARLY TO a cloudy Sunday morning. She sat up in bed and stretched. *Mmm, coffee, Mom's up.* She had just reached her bedroom door when she heard Rod's ring tone. "Hi Rod, you're up early too. I couldn't sleep, I'm so excited. Wait. What?"

"Eva has a migraine. I'm so sorry. I have to pick the boys up from camp. I hate to miss your show."

Eva has a migraine, Mim shouted in her head. "I'll be fine," she pressed "End." She grabbed her pillow in a chokehold and shook it, "Eva, Eva, Eva," then threw it across the room. She climbed into bed, pulling the covers over her head.

Mim felt her mom's weight on the bed. "Mim? Honey?" She didn't move. Irene waited. Finally, eyes swollen with tears, she turned toward her mother.

"Eva has a migraine," Mim choked back her tears, "Rod has to pick the boys up from camp." Irene hugged her daughter.

Mim pulled away, "I'm not going. What's the use if he won't be there?" She pulled the covers back over her head.

“I’ll ask Silkie if she can give me a ride.” Irene placed her hand on Mim’s shoulder, “Let me know if you change your mind.”

“Mim,” Irene called from the foyer, “Tom and Silkie are here.”

“Thanks for asking them to pick us up, Mom. I’m so nervous,” Mim said, adjusting her earring as she came down the hall.

Irene’s breath caught in her throat. “Oh, Honey,” she enveloped her daughter in a hug. Tom’s horn sounded.

“Two gorgeous women,” Silkie got out of the car to help Irene into the back seat and gave Mim a thumbs up.

Tom turned the corner to the Square and let out a holler. It looked like a festival. Colorful flags hung from the awning of Cactus Coffee. Helium balloons bobbed on the street corner. A sandwich board hung over a life-size paper mache figure welcoming people to “Art Show. Mim Rodriguez. Drawings of the Heart.”

Ali removed the orange cone as Tom pulled into the parking spot designated, “Guest of Honor.” Friends gathered in front of the shop: Ellen and Chet; Ralph, with his son and family; Don, Karyl, and Fred Stevens; Bob in his wheelchair in front of Addy and Joseph.

Tom opened Mim’s door and held his arm out to her. Silkie and Irene followed. Mim felt like a celebrity as Judith welcomed her and thanked everyone for coming. They clapped and cheered.

Mim was in her element as host of the exhibit. Friends and strangers congratulated her, exclaiming over her work. “You are so talented.” “Your drawings are so lifelike.”

The Lundys were there from the park campground. Velma took Mim aside. “You said you weren’t selling, Dear, but when you do, I would love this drawing of the park.”

The stained glass door of the coffee shop opened. Even with the bright sun in the background, Mim recognized the petite woman with the long gray hair, regal purple blouse and long skirt. “Silver Feather,” she whispered. Behind Silver Feather was the imposing figure of Frank Yazzie.

Mim was overcome with emotion. She felt Joseph’s hand on her elbow. “Your mother,” she said.

He smiled, “She makes a commanding entrance, doesn’t she?”

Silver Feather opened her arms to embrace Mim. Joseph bear-hugged his son and introduced Mim. She studied his face as he shook her hand, seeing the image in her portrait.

Bob wheeled his chair over, “I swear this must be heaven, a roomful of beautiful women.” Silver Feather leaned down and kissed his cheek. He offered his hand to Frank, “How’s my grandson?” Frank bent low to hug his grandfather. Bob took Silver Feather by the hand, “C’mon, you’re missing the show.”

Frank looked at Mim. “It’s nice to meet you. Grandmother says you’re a gifted artist. Much like a photographer I know.” He winked at his father. “Would you mind giving me a little tour?”

What did Bob say? This feels like heaven, Mim thought when Frank had let her go off to mingle among her guests. She glanced around the coffee shop. There was Chloe with Grandpa Fred, in front of the drawing of the Splash Pad. "Do Si Do," she said, threading her arm through his and twirling him around.

Addy was pondering the drawing of the figure slumped in the truck when Joseph walked up beside her. She looked up at him with tears in her eyes. He wrapped his arms around her.

"Join me for dinner?" she heard Ralph ask Irene. *Way to go, Mother.*

Out of the corner of her eye, Mim saw Silver Feather looking at a picture of Rod. She hurried over and said, "If you will wait here a moment, I have a surprise for you," and disappeared into the back room.

"Come with me, please." Silver Feather followed Mim to the back hallway. Mim posed her in front of the easel covered with a black cloth.

"May I present," Mim unveiled the portrait of Frank.

The old woman's eyes brimmed with tears. After a long moment, Silver Feather took Mim's hand, pulled her close, and whispered, "Thank you, My Daughter."

There was a tap on the door. "May I?" Joseph stepped inside and stared in awe at the portrait of his son.

After several moments, Addy knocked. "Mim," she stopped, speechless. Tears slipped down her cheeks. They stood together in a sacred moment before Addy recovered. "Your daughter's here."

"She came," Mim said.

"I told her you were back here with Joseph."

Mim opened the door to the crowded shop, her heart filled with joy. "Nini?"

"She and Luis were by the counter talking with Silkie," Addy said.

"Do you know what happened to Nini?" Mim looked around the exhibit.

Silkie shrugged, "She was right here. Next thing I knew, she grabbed Luis and vanished out the door."

Mim texted her, "I'm sorry I missed you. Please come back."

Mim sat on the patio that evening, basking in the magic of the day. The doorbell rang. Nini? She opened the door and slammed it. Realizing what she had done, she began laughing. The doorbell rang again.

"Mim," it was the voice of her nightmares, "open the door, please."

She took a deep breath and peeked out. There was Eva in a long dress, flawless make-up, dark mane flowing over her shoulders.

"You don't look like you have a migraine," Mim said.

"I need to talk to you," Eva said. "I should've done this years ago."

Mim maintained her vigil at the half-open door.

“Can I come in?”

“No, say what you have to say and go.” Eva huffed, Mim smiled inside.

“About today, I’m sorry. The boys had camp this weekend. Rod asked me to pick them up so he could go to your art show. I was so jealous; I made up the migraine.” She looked at her feet, then back at Mim. “I’ve only seen him this angry one other time.”

Mim’s interest was piqued, but she remained nonchalant. She leaned against the door.

“Mim, will you please let me in?”

Mim was seething at Eva’s manipulation. She wasn’t about to let this woman into her house. “Talk fast. I’m closing the door in three minutes.”

Eva’s jaw tightened, “We’ve never liked each other.” Mim tapped her foot. “When you divorced Rod, I was sure I had a chance with him. He was adamant he didn’t want more children, but I thought if I could give him a child, he would love me.”

Mim clenched her fists. She wanted to slam the door, but she had to know the story.

“When I told him I was pregnant, he was livid. I was almost afraid he might hurt me.”

“Rod would never...” Mim said.

“I know,” Eva held up her hand, “I was devastated. I couldn’t tell him I stopped taking my pills so I lied and said it must've been an accident." She paused and looked Mim in the eyes, "To this day, I have not told anyone."

Mim's stomach was in knots. This woman had ruined her life. She shook her head and put her hand on the doorknob.

Eva reached out. "He was almost as angry at me today," she said, "I could feel it. But it was the passion in his eyes I could see that he felt for you."

Mim glared at her.

"I've always despised that look. I wanted him to look at me that way. I'm certain what I did today extinguished any feeling he might have had. I am sorry, Mim. I'm not asking you to forgive me, but please forgive Rod."

Mim stared through the mirage in the fading evening light and closed the door. She returned to the patio. There was a voice message from Rod. "Hi, you must be busy. Call me when you have a chance. I love you."

I was busy all right, she thought. She sat at the empty table. No Nini. *Should I call her?* She pulled up "Favorites" and pressed Nini's number. No answer. Disheartened, Mim texted, "Nini, you have until Tuesday to decide if you are coming home or going to live with your dad."

Mim was drained when she climbed into bed. She felt the velvet pouch under her pillow and brushed it to the floor.

26

CACTUS COFFEE WAS BUSTLING on Monday morning with people full of compliments about the show. “Our resident artist.” “I’d love to see more of your work.” “You could sell those, you know.” *Mom, where are you when I need you?* Mim thought. She glanced at the Morning Men’s table. In the chaos she hadn’t realized the handsome man with the white beard was missing too.

At 8:05, the exercise ladies waltzed through the back door. Marie ordered a dark roast to go, “I’m off to my golf lesson,” she said, swinging an imaginary club in the air. “Wes and I loved the show.”

“May be the start of a new career, Frida,” Silkie teased.

Judith ordered lattes for her and Addy. “Thank you for everything you’ve done,” Mim said, ”coffee’s on me today.”

A short while later, Judith left to return the easels to the high school and Silkie headed back to her studio, leaving Addy alone at the table. Coffee pot in hand, Mim stopped by. “Thanks for coming to the show yesterday.”

“Thank you,” she said, ”your work touched my heart. The truck,” the women exchanged a knowing look, “and the portrait of Frankie.” Her face beamed with a mother’s love.

Tears sparkled in her blue eyes, “You’re wasting your gift here.”

Mim scrunched her eyebrows. “Funny you should say that. Last night I dreamed I was back in the classroom teaching art.”

Addy looked into Mim’s eyes. “Silver Feather would say your dreams are sending you a message. Listen.”

27

THE BLENDER WAS WHIRRING when Mim opened the front door. She stood in the hallway, staring at her phone. Irene peeked around the corner. Mim's shoulders sagged. "I was hoping to hear from Nini. I sent her an ultimatum on Sunday."

Ultimatum? Irene wondered. "I made margaritas," she said. "If you want to grab the chips and salsa, we can sit outside. I just wiped off the chairs and table from last night's rain." Mim followed her mother to the patio. It was still overcast but warm. They settled into the wicker chairs. "Tell me about this ultimatum," Irene said.

Mim took a sip of her frosty drink. "I've made such a mess of my life, Mom. I've spent so much time waiting, waiting for somebody to rescue me. But after my art show I realized I can do this. I need to do this."

Irene raised her glass in agreement.

"Drawing is my passion. I'm just like Dad. It's in my blood. I was so alive yesterday. I wanted Rod and Nini to be there, but they weren't. So I did it myself. It broke my heart that Nini left before she even spoke to me. I sent her an ultimatum and expected her reply by today."

"You haven't heard anything," Irene said. Mim shook her head. "I'd like to make a toast. To you," Irene lifted her glass. "You inspire me with your strength, your warmth, your talent." They clicked glasses. "To your dreams coming true."

Mim grinned. "Sunday night I dreamed I was teaching again. I woke up feeling like it was telling me something. I'm going to talk to Tom and see if he knows of any art jobs out there."

Mim's phone buzzed. She looked at her mom before she picked it up and looked at the message. She shook her head and frowned.

"Maybe a little walk before dinner would do you good," Irene said.

Mim took a deep breath. "That may be just what I need. Care to join me?"

"You go ahead. I'll clean up here and have the tacos ready when you get back."

Mim kissed the top of her mom's head. "Thanks, I love you."

Irene put the glasses on the tray. She picked up the bowl of chips and saw Mim's phone was beside it. "5:05," it read.

Mim drove to Soaring Eagle and passed the lot at the Education Center. She decided to hike the Mesquite Trail where she had gone with Joseph. She looked for his truck. *He must've gone home already,* she thought.

Flashlight and water bottle in hand, she headed up the path. She took a deep breath, feeling the warmth of the sun on her face. *I love the desert after a storm,* she thought. She planned a good hour's walk out past the clearing where she and Joseph had watched the night sky and back. Dusk would be falling when she returned.

Irene finished preparing the tacos and sat down to watch the news while she waited for Mim. *She's taking a longer walk than I expected,* Irene thought when the news ended. She went to the kitchen to stir the meat simmering on the stove and looked out at the orange glow of the evening sky.

By seven it was dark and Mim had not returned. *I don't want to be silly, but what if something has happened to her?* Irene thought. *No need to alarm Rod. Joseph might still be working. I'll call Silkie. She'll know what to do.*

Hearing Silkie's voice was reassuring. "She probably ran into someone and didn't realize the time," Silkie said. "I'll check with Joseph and call you back. I bet she's on her way now."

Irene walked out to the driveway, hoping Mim's car would appear. *She's going to be upset with me for getting all worked up about this,* Irene thought. *She just went for a walk.* Irene saw headlights coming down the street. Her phone rang. "Thank you, Silkie, Ralph's here. Has Joseph seen Mim?"

"No, Tom went to meet him at the park. I thought you might like some company. Try to stay calm, Irene. I'm sure everything will be okay."

“I have an idea which trail she took,” Joseph told Tom as he sped along the park road, ignoring the 15 MPH sign. “If I told you I think she’s fine, I’d be lying.”

Up ahead in the pull-off, they spotted Mim’s SUV. They grabbed the flashlights and hurried toward the trail following the random footprints in the mud.

“Mim,” they called into the still night. “Mim, can you hear me?”

“Please Lord,” Joseph prayed, “let her be safe.”

The men spotted her at the same time. She lay face up, a halo of wavy chestnut hair around her face. “Mim, can you hear me? Mim?” Joseph knelt beside her, “She’s breathing.”

Before he could tell Tom to call 911, he heard him on the phone, “We need an ambulance at Soaring Eagle State Park. A woman has fallen. She’s unresponsive. We are at...”

Joseph felt Tom’s hand on his shoulder. “The ambulance is on its way. I told Silkie and Irene to meet us at the hospital. Should we call Rod?”

“Let’s wait until the ambulance gets here. We’ll know more then.”

Tom went back down the trail. Soon sirens blared and rotating lights filled the darkness. Joseph knelt in the mud beside Mim and stroked her hair. “Help is coming. Stay with me. You saved my life once. Let me pay you back.”

The EMTs descended upon them with their medical bags and a stretcher. From the marks in the mud, it looked like she had tripped and fallen, breaking her leg and hitting her head on a rock. She moaned as they moved her onto the stretcher.

In the truck, following the ambulance, Tom asked about the call to Rod. "I didn't think about what it would look like to him. I only know he's the one person Mim would want to be there. When he questioned me, I just said we were on our way to the hospital."

Joseph parked in the Emergency Room lot and he and Tom followed the stretcher into the hospital. Silkie, Addy, Irene, and Ralph, met them in the waiting room.

"Thank you, Joseph," Irene rushed to him, "where did you find her? I feel so guilty. I should have called earlier. I should have gone with her. This is all my fault."

"You probably saved her life, Irene," Joseph said.

Irene kept her eyes on the entrance waiting for Rod. Time seemed to drag. Finally the doors swooshed open and he strode in. She went to greet him.

"What happened? Where is she?" He looked past Joseph to Tom.

"She's been in there over an hour. I'm sure we'll hear..."

The ER doors swung open. The group stood as a woman in scrubs came toward them, her face noncommittal. They feared the worst.

"How is she?" Rod said.

"She broke her tibia," the doctor said, motioning to her lower leg, "and sustained a concussion. We've sedated her to keep her still. She's lucky you found her when you did."

Joseph glanced at Irene.

"How long will she have to stay?" Silkie stood beside Rod.

"Two or three days. We'll monitor her overnight and see how she's doing in the morning. Are you her sister?"

Silkie shook her head. "No, but this is her husband."

"Ex-husband," Rod said.

"Do you have power of attorney?"

"No, but I..."

The doctor looked around at the anxious faces. "Who is her closest relative?"

"Her mother is here," Joseph motioned to Irene.

"Come with me," the doctor said. "It will be best for the rest of you to go home."

Rod was exhausted when he arrived at Mim's. The kitchen smelled of tacos, the meat in the pan on the stove, ready for dinner.

He started down the hallway. *Irene's probably staying in the guest room. I'll stay in Nini's room. Nini,* he thought, *I need to tell Nini.* He pulled out his cell phone. 10:30. *It's late. I'll call her in the morning, maybe take her to breakfast.*

He opened the bedroom door. Framed pictures and drawings were stacked around the room. His heart tightened. Mim's art show. How could he have missed it? He closed his eyes. *What if?* The doctor had said she would be okay.

He walked slowly to Mim's room. The door was ajar and her shirt and khakis lay on the floor by the closet. He set his overnight bag beside the unmade bed, took off his clothes, and slid beneath the cool sheets. He thought about the last time he had been in this bed. *What if?* He thought of the woman he loved, the texture of her hair, the curves of her body, the musky smell of her soft skin. He fell asleep thinking he would never take her for granted again.

28

ROD WAS SURPRISED TO see Addy in the Intensive Care Unit. He didn't know she was hospital staff. He waved to Irene through the window of Mim's room. He couldn't see much, but it looked like Mim was sleeping.

"Rod?" Addy said, "looks like Mim had a quiet night. They're waiting for the doctor to make his rounds."

He nodded at her staff ID, "Is there any way you can get me in to see her?"

"The hospital has strict rules," she said, "let me see what I can do." The staff neurologist came down the hall. "Good morning, Dr. Wu." Addy smiled at Rod and followed the doctor into Mim's room.

Moments later, Addy and Irene appeared. Irene hugged Rod, "Did you get any sleep last night?"

"I was up most of the night. Maybe it was the tacos you left me."

"Oh goodness, the tacos."

Rod grinned, "What did the doctor say?"

"He had a brief look at her chart," Addy said. "Irene told him she woke up for a moment this morning, moaned, and went back to sleep. Dr. Wu will be back to see her when he's had more time to review her chart. I'd better get back to the floor. Here's my cell number if you need me."

"Irene, can I run you home?" Rod said.

"Thanks, but,"

Ralph strode around the corner. "Good morning," his eyes twinkled as he put his arm around Irene. "How's Mim doing this morning?"

"I just told the doctor she slept pretty well."

"I bet you didn't," he took her elbow, "let me get you home."

An older woman holding a Bible sat next to a man, perhaps her son, near the window in the waiting room. Rod settled into a stiff vinyl chair and opened the book he had brought, but could only stare at Mim's room.

A nurse in pale blue scrubs, her gray hair in a bun atop her head, pushed a cart into Mim's room. She didn't appear to be in a hurry so Rod was not alarmed. Moments later, she gave a discerning look in Rod's direction as she left.

"I figured I'd find you here," it was Silkie, carrying a flower arrangement and a tote stuffed with cards. "She's got quite the fan club. I found these in front of the coffee shop." She kissed his cheek. "How are you?"

Rod wrapped his arms around her and held on to her like a lifeline. He stepped back and wiped the tears from his eyes.

"I could use a cup of coffee," Silkie motioned toward the pot in the waiting room. "Can I get you one?"

Mim's head was pounding. Addy? Her lips were moving.

"hoping you'd be awake. I want to thank you for inspiring me."

"My head," Mim winced.

Addy stroked Mim's arm, "You're in the ICU. You fell and banged your head pretty good and broke your leg," she lifted the blanket revealing the cast.

"Hit my head?" Mim looked up at the monitors. Nothing was making sense.

"Do you remember going for a walk at the park?" Mim nodded. "You slipped and fell. Tom and Joseph found you. You're doing better now. I think they're going to move you to another floor."

"What are you doing here?" Mim said.

"I came to thank you. I'm going to see my mother, to show her this." Addy raised her left hand.

Silver Feather's ring. *When a mother accepts her son's choice of a wife.* "Oh Addy," Mim said, "you and Joseph?"

She beamed. "I've lived in fear of my mother my whole life. She's a monster. People love her but they have no idea. She's so controlling, made life miserable for my dad and me. When I got pregnant and my dad took me to the reservation, she left him. A blessing really," Addy smirled. "But she refused to grant him a divorce. And she said if I ever married 'that savage' that she would see to it that I never worked in medicine again. And I knew her well enough not to call her bluff. Until now." Addy looked at the ring. "You inspired me. I'm driving to Albuquerque after work to show her my ring."

Addy heard Dolores talking to Rod and Silkie as she left Mim's room. "All right," the older woman scanned the hallway, "looks pretty clear, let's go."

It took Mim a moment before she recognized the large figure in the sterile gown, cap, and mask. "Rod," she held out her hand to take his.

His eyes smiled above the mask as he kissed her bandaged head. "You scared us," he sat on the edge of the bed. She gave him a half smile, drowsy from the pain medicine. "Rest now," he said, "I'll be here when you wake up."

The doctor came in an hour later. Mim's concussion was not as severe as they had feared and they were moving her to the med/surg floor to monitor her there, hoping to discharge her tomorrow. Rod was relieved.

Dolores returned with a tech. Rod gathered her things and followed them to the elevator. Once in the unit, Rod called Irene and Silkie with the update. Then he texted Nini: "Mom out of ICU. Want to see her?"

Mim was tired by early evening. Silkie, Tom, and Judith had stopped. Rhonda popped in during a break from the Radiology Clinic. Mim was ready to sleep so she sent Rod and Irene home to rest because she would need their care when she returned home tomorrow. Irene left Mim's phone on the stand insisting she call if she needed them.

Rod took Irene to El Corral for dinner and a margarita, which tasted so good after the stress of the past two days. When they got home, Irene retired to her room.

As Rod passed Nini's room his attention was drawn to the pictures from the art show. There was a beautiful desert scene against the pillow on the bed and one of him in his baseball uniform. In the ornate silver frame behind it was Mim's gift to him on their first anniversary, their wedding dance. He was overcome with the same love he felt for his bride that day. He glimpsed the matted drawing behind it. His heart caught in his throat. Their totem, the soaring eagles, restored. He carried it down the hall to Mim's room.

Rod dropped his shirt and jeans in a pile on the floor beside the bed and looked again at the soaring eagles in the spotlight beneath the lamp. Feeling powerless, he pulled back the comforter, exposing a small white pouch on the floor beside the nightstand, FOREVER embroidered below two eagles, their wings overlapping. His heart stopped. The pouch he had had made to hold the engagement ring he had presented to her after a romantic dinner at Peaceful Pines. His heart thudded as he untied the ribbons of the pouch. There, glistening, Mim's engagement and wedding rings. He threw his clothes back on and left a note in the kitchen, "Irene, Spending night with Mim."

Rod walked down the dimly lit hallway of the third floor to Mim's room hoping she would be awake. He opened the door and stopped.

Joseph sat by Mim's side holding her hand. "I've been waiting for you," he rose and came toward Rod, extending his hand. "She's been sleeping fitfully. She keeps calling your name."

Mim stirred. "Rosie, wait."

Rod blinked, his head resting on the back of the chair beside Mim's bed, legs outstretched. He leaned forward and shook her shoulder, "Mim, it's okay. I'm here."

She opened her eyes. "Rod," she clutched his hand, "I saw Rosie."

"You must have been dreaming again," he said.

Mim heard Rosie's sweet little voice in her heart,

"Wake up, Mom.

I love you.

Step out.

I am walking beside you."

29

GRACE OPENED THE FRONT door, shielding her eyes from the sun. "Mr. Begay," she said.

"Hi Grace, is Nini here?"

"She's busy."

Nini appeared behind her, "Mr. Begay."

"Your dad called and asked me to bring you to the hospital. He wants you there to bring your mom home. I think he texted you."

Home, Nini thought of the text she had sent. "My father called you? Why would he...?" A loud barking sounded from the driveway. Bandit bounded around the corner of the garage. "Bandit," Nini hugged him.

"Shall we go now?" Joseph said.

Nini looked at Grace and nodded.

"Up, Boy," Joseph signaled Bandit to take his place in the back of the truck. The German shepherd pranced past him and stood by the cab door. "Just like old times," he opened the door and Bandit leaped in, with Nini behind him.

"You saved my mom's life," Nini looked up from her phone, "thank you."

"No need to thank me. Let's just get your mom home." He pulled around the circular drive of the hospital.

Nini squirmed. "You're not coming in?"

She was nervous as she went to the elevator and rode to the third floor. She had not seen her mom since their walk. She had run away from the art show. And all because she jumped to conclusions. She shuffled down the hallway and peeked into Mim's room.

Her mom and dad were laughing, Mim's cast propped up on Rod's lap. "Nini," they greeted her.

Nini hugged Rod. Mim picked up the cell phone in her lap. "I got your message."

"Mom, I," Nini stammered, "I'm so sorry. When I sent it I didn't know..."

Mim looked at the phone. "I understand," she said, "it's okay."

"Okay? You want me to go live with Dad?"

"It's the only way it will work," Mim said. She held out her hand, "because I'll be living with him, too." The engagement ring sparkled as Mim gathered her family in her arms, "Let's go home."

READER'S EXPERIENCE

Dear Reader,

Each of us is on our own unique journey. There is no roadmap. What an incredible experience I have had writing this book. It is my hope that you have had an enlightening experience reading it.

Here are some thoughts to ponder:

1. I'd love to meet...at Cactus Coffee to talk about...
2. I laughed out loud when...
3. I got teary when...
4. The character I relate to most is...because...
5. My "Soaring Eagle State Park," the place where I go to find solace is...
6. A dream I'd like to fulfill is...
7. I'd like to ask you, the author...

I'd love to meet you at a coffee shop one day and sit down for a chat.

Until then,

Karin

Acknowledgments

Heartfelt thanks to family and friends who have supported me on this journey. Special thanks to:

The Sunshine Corner, Sarah and Lexi, for your guiding spirit from the book's conception to the final words and beyond. Ever grateful.

My editor, Michael Cutler, for your insight and commitment to my story.

My great-niece, Jenna Cutler, for your enthusiasm for writing which has inspired me throughout the creation of this book.

My mentor, Alan Watt, of the l.a. writers' lab, for your dedication to our craft and for helping me bring to life the story within.

The writers at the Ojai Retreat and my Tuscany Tribe for your invaluable input and encouragement.

My friend, Ellen Frank, for the magic of Little Green Truck Coffee in Auburn, Iowa.

My dear friends: Deb Gute, Patty Lusero, Amy Fordyce, Nan Janis, and Kathy Hodges, for your time and input in the manuscript, blurb, and readers' experience.

My family. My husband of forty-one years, Ed, for your unconditional love and support. Our sons: Mike, Dan, Andy, and Kenny. Their spouses: Erin, Jamie, and Amanda. Our grandchildren: Olivia, Vincent, Jackson, Kaylee, Madelyn, Ed, and Julian. Together we can accomplish anything. It's what we do. I love you with all my heart.

ABOUT THE AUTHOR

KARIN CUTLER retired as an educator in 2016, excited about a future that had no map. As a military spouse, Karin moved around the country with her husband and four sons. Their lives have been blessed by the friendships they made and adventures they had everywhere they went.

Karin's favorite things are connecting with people at the local coffee shop and gathering women to scheme and dream. Her mother once told her, "Honey, I thought you'd be the one (of my seven children) to write a book." So she did. Karin is delighted to present her debut novel, The Image of Me.

Connect with Karin at kscutler51@gmail.com

Made in the USA
Lexington, KY
03 December 2019